WENDY DAY

Mexico, Margaritas, and Murder

*The delightful laugh-out-loud mystery adventure
featuring best friends Sally and Pearl*

OPEN SKY
PUBLISHING

First edition

ISBN: 978-1-957707-13-6

This book was professionally typeset on Reedsy.
Find out more at reedsy.com

Dedicated to
Grandma Sally Craig, who shows love in every stitch, makes my favorite cookies, and is the best-dressed woman I know.

Great-grandma Pearl Lynn, who taught me to play Checkers, introduced me to Jesus, and never took crap from anyone.

Contents

1

A Sticky Situation

Sally focused on two things as she crouched down behind the pallet of boxes. First, she wasn't ready to die; second, she really needed to pee. "You've got to get us out of here," she whispered through clenched teeth.

Her best friend, Pearl, licked her lips and said in a gravelly southern accent, "You could help, you know. I ain't the only one hooked on true crime. Thought you'd have a plan by now."

"When was I supposed to make a plan?" Sally asked, her knees crackling and dust tickling her nose. Sally had no idea where they were, and she could have kicked herself for not finishing her Spanish lessons before coming to Mexico. Now they were being chased, and Sally was about to wet her pants. This was precisely what her kids had worried would happen.

"Shhh. I hear somebody talkin' outside. Come here," Pearl said, motioning for Sally to move closer to the back wall behind another stack of boxes. "Scoot down lower. You teased your hair too high. It's stickin' up like a rooster and gonna get us killed."

"I can't scoot down that low. I won't be able to get back up."

"Just do what I'm doin'," Pearl whispered.

"You're a foot closer to the ground than I am," Sally whispered back.

The door to the warehouse creaked, and a sliver of sunlight spread across the floor. Sally's heart pounded in her ears. Pearl grabbed her hand and squeezed it so tight that her fingers went numb. What were they going to do? Maybe the warehouse had been a dumb idea, but it seemed like the best option after escaping the back of the van.

"Hello. Anybody in here?"

Sally's stomach dropped. She knew that voice.

"Oh, my stars," Pearl whispered and rolled her eyes.

Sally turned to look behind them. Spotting a door in the corner, she whispered, "We're going to have to make a run for it."

"I can hear you talking. You're not that quiet, you know," the voice called out.

Sally strained to pinpoint where the voice was in the warehouse. If they wanted to get to the door, they would have to cross a wide opening between the stacks of boxes. If they ran, they could reach it. But if the door was locked, they were sunk.

Maybe they should give up. They could talk it out. Sally locked her knees together and bit her lip. Who was she kidding? That person couldn't be reasoned with.

"You can come out. It's okay. This was all just a misunderstanding." The voice was farther away than it had been before.

Sally perked up. Now was their chance. She squeezed Pearl's hand and pointed to the door. Pearl gave her a quick nod. Sally leaned close to Pearl's ear and whispered, "Let's go. On the count of three."

"Come on, girls, let's grab a drink and talk it out."

Sally put up her fingers.

One.

Two.

Three.

Sally took a deep breath and ran, pulling Pearl along after her. They crossed between two pallets of boxes before there was a sharp call from the other side of the building. "Hey!"

"Crap," Pearl panted as they ran.

"Keep moving," Sally said without looking back.

"If I have a heart attack, I'm gonna kill you."

A loud crack rang out, and glass rained from a window above. They both shrieked, Sally's ears ringing. "What was that?" she asked.

"Gunshot."

Sally's steps faltered, but Pearl grabbed her elbow and pulled her along. A gunshot? Sally had never heard a gunshot in real life.

"Faster," Pearl cried. They were twenty feet from the door.

Another gunshot hit a stack of boxes next to them.

Hold on. How did two small-town seniors get themselves into this situation? Maybe we should start at the end.

2

The End

Friday, June 3rd

Sally Johnson sat perched on the edge of a red velvet chair, twisting the tissue in her hands into a rope until it shredded before stuffing it into her jacket pocket. The pointy-nosed funeral director pressed his lips together and leaned forward on his mahogany desk, folding his hands. "Mrs. Johnson, it simply isn't done."

Sally had known the funeral director for his entire life and his father before him. If his father hadn't retired last year to Florida, none of this would be an issue. She exhaled through her nose and spoke with only a hint of a quiver. "Harold was a side sleeper his entire life. His eternal rest should be on his side as well." Sally looked down at the desk. A small chip in the corner seemed out of place in the tidy office. She pulled at the hem of her blazer. She needed to stay strong.

The funeral director leaned back and straightened his blue tie. "Alright, I'm sure we can find a solution," he sniffed. The desk drawer scraped against the track as he opened it and pulled out a yellow notepad. Retrieving a pen from the inside pocket of his suit coat, he tapped it on the paper, thinking. "Maybe we could put him on his side for the open casket portion of the service and then roll him onto his back before we close the lid?"

"Oh, I don't know." Sally lifted her eyes to meet his and said shakily, "I don't want to cause trouble, but we were married for 46 years. When I said I wanted him on his side, I meant for eternity, not just for the funeral."

"Of course." The funeral director cleared his throat and excused himself, buttoning his suit coat on his way out the door. When he returned, a disheveled-looking younger man followed. He introduced himself as the mortician, and after Sally repeated her demand, he sat in the chair next to hers, "Ma'am, I understand that this is a hard time for you. There are some logistical issues with your request."

When Sally stared at him, he continued. "He won't fit in a casket on his side."

"There has to be some way." Sally's lip quivered. "He was always so peaceful when he was sleeping. I want to remember him like that." When they were younger, she would sometimes lay in bed, wide awake, and watch his slow breathing. She'd liked to think he would be like that forever.

"The dimensions of the casket don't allow for that. He simply won't fit." The mortician paused, sighing, and ran a hand through his hair. "I guess maybe there's something we could do."

Sally looked up, hopeful. "Anything. I don't care what it is." She pulled another tissue out of her purse and blew her nose.

The mortician folded his arms and tapped his chin with a finger. "I don't mean to be blunt, but I am not sure how else to say this." He took a deep breath through his nose. "I would have to break his shoulders." He cracked his knuckles and looked at Sally.

The funeral director's face went ashen, and he cleared his throat.

Sally dabbed her eyes and considered. "I'm fine with that."

After a beat, the mortician leaned forward with a finger in the air. "Nope. Unfortunately that isn't the only issue, so that's not all it would take to make this work. You would also need to purchase the deluxe-sized casket to put him on his side, which costs extra."

The two men in the room looked at each other and then back at her. Sally clutched the hem of her jacket. She couldn't afford the more expensive casket. Tears filled her eyes, and she blinked them back.

The funeral director glared at the mortician, and a silent conversation unfolded between them. Finally, the funeral director cleared his throat and said, "Mrs. Johnson, I apologize for my colleague's insensitivity. My father always spoke highly of you and your family." He glanced at a framed photo of his father sitting on the credenza. "Tell you what. We can upgrade you to a deluxe casket at no charge and lay Harold on his side." He looked down over his glasses at the mortician. "Without breaking anything."

The mortician shrugged, "Okay then, side sleeper it is." The funeral director shot him a stern look, and the mortician skittered out of the room.

Sally smiled. Pearl would be proud of her.

3

He Looks Orange

Monday, June 6th

Three days later, Sally crossed her ankles under the padded black folding chair next to the coffin. The funeral director had ushered her to this spot so she could greet mourners, like it was an honor to sit beside a dead body and smile at people she barely knew.

She tried to be gracious. But after two hours, she was tired and only wanted to go home. People kept commenting on his side sleeper setup, assuming it was a mistake. She didn't have the energy to explain it, so she just bit her lip and tried to ignore them.

When there was a lull in the stream of mourners, she glanced over at Harold, her husband of 46 years. *He looks orange.* Someone had caked on the makeup, including lipstick. A laugh caught in her throat. She covered her mouth with the back of her hand and faked a cough. He would be so mad.

Instead, he was peacefully lying on his side, dressed in a dark navy suit. Five days ago, he had been yelling at the television again when he'd just slumped over in his tattered plaid recliner. It had been quite dramatic with the paramedics and coroner at the house. All of the neighbors had wandered onto their lawns, craning their necks to catch a glimpse of poor dead Harold as he'd been wheeled out on a stretcher.

She had watched it all unfold like some out-of-body experience. She barely remembered pulling open the door with tears on her face. She had watched them rip open his shirt and try to restart his heart as she'd stood by helplessly. At one point, she had offered a paramedic a beverage. Her entire body had been numb.

"Ma'am, is there anyone you can call?" A police officer with kind brown eyes had asked .

The cell phone in her hand had hung heavy at her side as she'd nodded. She had sat in the plaid recliner and made the calls. The kids had been devastated, of course. Now they sat huddled in the front row with their families to comfort them, and she sat next to Harold. She was relieved when the funeral director ushered her to a chair in the front row next to her oldest daughter, Lauren.

Why did they always make the family sit front and center? Sally felt like she was on display. She didn't want all these people watching her. She looked down at her hands and then picked a piece of lint off her sleeve. The designer pantsuit had been hanging in her closet since she'd found it at the Baptist church bag sale. It was her best find yet. She hadn't been sure if she should wear it, with the sheer sleeves and flowing pants, but Lauren had encouraged her, saying it made her look classy and refined.

After the pastor from her church said a few words, which were awkward and vague as this was the first time Harold had been inside a church in years, Lauren stood up. God bless that girl. She had offered to give the eulogy. Sally had held her emotions together all day, stoic in her role as a widow. As Lauren talked, silent tears started to fall, and Sally had to dig through her purse for tissues to keep her nose from running all over the place.

Death was a funny thing. In the shadow of loss, bad memories and negative traits seemed to blur-maybe it was all the crying.

Lauren talked about her dad's best parts and how much he adored his little girl. It was a lovely speech. She included just the right amount of humor and tenderness. Then they all stood to sing.

During the final verse of "Amazing Grace," Sally was led back down the aisle. She blinked rapidly to force the moisture back into her stinging eyes. She scanned the chapel as she walked. There was a respectable crowd. There weren't many family members in attendance, as Harold was an only child, and her only brother had moved his family to London for work years ago, never to return. Harold's old coworkers from the factory were there, but she didn't know most of them, only recognizing who they were because of the silver Ford pins they wore on their lapels. Several other men might have been from Harold's bowling league some years ago, but Sally had never met them.

After the appropriate kind words were said, Harold was lowered into his side sleeping eternity at the cemetery next to the church. Then the small crowd moved on to the multi-purpose room for a luncheon prepared by the church auxiliary.

Sally sat at a round table covered with a white linen cloth. Her body had dropped into the chair, and protested at the idea of getting up for the buffet line. She wasn't hungry anyway.

A few minutes later, Lauren placed a plate of fried chicken and green beans in front of her. Sally managed a weak smile and thanked her daughter, even though she hadn't asked for food and wasn't confident she could hold anything down.

Sally picked at her plate, pushing the food around and eating a few bites of the fried chicken. It stuck in her throat like sandpaper. Her stomach roiled, and she pushed her plate away. While Lauren coaxed her daughter into eating a spoonful of peas, Sally stood to take the food to the trash can.

Lauren looked up from her task. "Mom, are you sure you don't want us to come back to the house? You shouldn't be alone." One of the peas rolled off the spoon and escaped across the floor. Lauren bent down to grab it.

"Whatever works best for you. I don't want to be a bother," Sally smiled halfheartedly. "But I would never turn down a visit from you."

Sally's youngest son, Henry, sat over at the next table with his wife. He turned to Sally and said, "Our flight leaves in three hours. I can change it if you don't want to be alone."

Sally smiled sadly. Henry had his father's brown eyes and long lashes. He slipped off his well-tailored suit jacket and folded it over the back of his chair. Henry had always been an overachiever and was currently a lawyer in Dallas. Despite the offer, Sally knew he needed to return to the office.

Joel, her middle son, walked over with a plate piled high with fried chicken and scalloped potatoes. He was a computer programmer in Seattle. His partner, Tom, had a big presentation at work and couldn't come back for the funeral. Joel used his forearm to push his bangs out of his eyes and said, "Mom, you shouldn't be alone; it isn't safe until you change the locks in the house and get an alarm system." He slid into a chair next to Lauren.

"Mom lives in the most boring town in Michigan," Henry said, breaking off a piece of a dinner roll.

Joel pointed his fork at Henry. "There is crime everywhere."

"Stop trying to scare mom," Henry chided.

"I'm just being realistic."

"What are you going to do when you get home?" Lauren asked Sally, abandoning the peas and handing her small daughter a dinner roll, which the child greedily snatched and started eating.

Sally could have kissed Lauren for interrupting the bickering. She slipped the tear-stained funeral program into her purse. "I don't know. Probably watch a few episodes of my shows and go to bed. It's been a long day. I'll be fine, though."

"Are you sure? We could come and play cards or watch a movie, something more uplifting than true crime."

Sally leaned down to kiss Lauren's forehead. "You're a good daughter." Then she turned to her boys. "Stop worrying about me. You both have planes to catch, and I can care for myself."

Henry nodded. Joel shook his head and stabbed his fork into his pile of potatoes. Lauren looked at her husband, who was wrestling with their three-year-old, long overdue for a nap. "Okay, but if you need anything, please call, and I'll come."

"I will," said Sally, circling to kiss her granddaughter and son-in-law on the cheek.

Sally drove home to the respectable three-bedroom, two-bathroom ranch she'd shared with Harold for 40 years. The leather stitching on the steering wheel dug into her cheek as she rested her head, trying to summon the energy to go into the empty house.

After standing in the doorway and letting her mind adjust to the silence, she slipped off her shoes. There was a knock at the front door. She cracked it open, and her best friend Pearl stood outside, curly hair more blue than platinum, holding a dish covered in foil. "I've been sittin' in my car for two hours waitin' for you to get home. I almost had to break into the pie to keep my blood sugar from droppin' out and killin' me."

Sally gave a half-smile and stepped back, allowing Pearl to enter. Pearl was the one person she did want to see right now. She wouldn't fuss or expect Sally to fuss.

"You could've come to the funeral," Sally said.

Pearl kicked off her shoes, "Oh sweetie, you know I would have. But I don't like to speak ill of the dead. And I ain't gettin' that close to a coffin. I got one foot in the grave already. Don't need to fall in accidentally." She dropped her purse onto Harold's chair and turned to face Sally. "Now, friend, I know your heart feels like it's been rode hard and put up wet. I'm here for you. We can talk about it or not. We can play cards, eat all this pie, or I can run down to the corner store and buy some tequila, and we can get drunk and watch that new documentary about the Mud Bog murders. You choose."

Sally's eyes welled up with tears, and she laughed. "I am so glad you're here."

4

Get Out of Bed

Monday, June 20th

Sally ran a hand over her tangled, greasy hair. Ugh. She hadn't showered in days. Her heart ached with something she couldn't quite explain. She knew she was grieving, but it was complicated.

Her marriage to Harold had started off promising but had gradually given way to a tense, critical environment. He'd worked hard, come home stressed, and never had learned to manage his temper. But still, he'd been a constant presence in her life, even if she'd spent most of her time moving out of his way.

Her daughter Lauren had been checking on her every day. She'd taken on sorting through papers and caring for loose ends. Sally had never felt strong, but Lauren was a rock. Ever since she was little, she'd never been afraid of anything, even her dad. After college, the boys had moved out of state. Sally was glad they'd returned for the funeral, even if they had left for home shortly afterward. Maybe she should have asked them to stay.

Now the house was quiet as she lay in bed. She turned over to face where Harold had slept. The bedding was still tucked in on his side. She slid her foot back and forth under the sheets. She pulled up the blankets and rolled over onto his side of the mattress. She tried to get comfortable but kept slipping into the indention left by his body after years of sleeping in the same position. She gave up and rolled back to her side, pulling his pillow to her chest. She hurt, not only because he was gone, but because he never learned to be the kind of husband she needed. Now, what was she going to do?

She sighed and looked at the ceiling, her eyes traveling to the dusty ceiling fan blades. She should probably get out of bed. But why? No one needed her to make lunch. Maybe she'd just stay in bed forever.

She heard the front door slam shut. Pearl called out a greeting, then padded down the hall to the bedroom. She appeared in the doorway wearing tan Bermuda shorts, sandals, and a purple top with sequins along the neckline. "Honey, you got to get out of the house. It's been three weeks, and you ain't gone anywhere."

Sally pulled the pastel comforter up under her chin and turned her head away from Pearl, leaning against the door frame with her hand on her hip. "I'm a grieving widow. I'm allowed to stay at home and do nothing."

Pearl waved her off and walked in to sit on the edge of the bed. "Hogwash. You can't just sit in this room and wither away to nothin'."

Sally pulled her arms from the blanket and folded them. "Oh, I don't know."

Pearl leaned over and patted her hand. "I know you're sad.

14

You can stay sad, but you gotta get up."

Sally sniffed. "I don't know what I am supposed to do. I used to be a wife and a mother. Now my kids are grown, and Harold is gone." She had been proud to be a wife and mother. She'd been a classroom mom and had volunteered to make cookies for her husband's friends at work each Christmas.

"Well, that's exactly why you gotta find out. You gotta get out of this bed and explore the great beyond." Pearl waved a hand in front of her as if she was painting a picture of what could be.

"I wouldn't even know where to start. I haven't done anything or gone anywhere." Sally used her feet to push herself up against the oak headboard and grabbed a tissue from the box on the nightstand, blowing her nose loudly. The only places she and Harold had ever traveled were to the Grand Canyon when the kids were little, and a quick trip to Orlando for their twenty-fifth wedding anniversary.

Pearl clapped her hands together. "I don't mean no offense, but Harold was so cheap he wouldn't give a nickel to see Jesus ridin' a bicycle. You need a trip."

Sally chuckled and wrinkled her nose. What was Pearl talking about? "A trip? To where? I can't afford that." Sally had never worked, except for a part-time job at the local flower shop. She hadn't let herself consider what she would do for money now. Her daughter was still going through the piles of papers on Harold's dresser, and while Lauren had assured her she wouldn't be homeless no matter what it all added up to, she likely didn't have much money to spare.

"I know you got life insurance money. You can take a little bit of that and take yourself on a trip. I know the perfect place." Pearl stood up and danced around in a circle, wiggling her hips.

"Mexico."

Sally laughed and covered her mouth with the back of her hand. She did have a check sitting on the kitchen counter, waiting to be cashed. She sighed, threw the blanket back, and swung her feet to the floor. "I can't go to Mexico. I've never even been out of the country."

Pearl took her hand and pulled her to her feet. "First time for everythin'." Sally straightened her pajama top and pushed the tangles out of her face.

"You need coffee. Come on." Pearl led her into the cheery kitchen at the back of the house. After watching a decorating show on television, Sally had painted the walls yellow and the cabinets white. A vase of artificial sunflowers sat in the middle of the small round wooden breakfast table. A coordinating wallpaper border wrapped the room. It was Sally's favorite room in the house.

But the usually spotless kitchen was currently a cluttered mess. Wilting and dead flower arrangements covered the counter. The sink was full of cereal bowls. Sally had gone through two boxes of granola, despite the fridge being full of casseroles and meals from her friends. She hadn't had the energy to reheat anything.

"I've never been out of the country. I wouldn't even know what to pack," Sally said, perched on her white kitchen chair.

Pearl turned on the coffee pot and reached up on her tiptoes into the cupboard for a filter and a can of coffee grounds. "We'll get you right as rain. The perfect excuse to go shoppin'." She turned around and smiled. "And I do love shoppin'. Now stop worryin'. After we get some coffee in you, we are goin' to get lunch and make a plan."

"Oh, I don't know."

Pearl ignored her. "Oh, and we are goin' to bingo this week. It's been too long, and I don't want anyone stealin' our seats."

Sally thought about the first time she had met Pearl. It'd been at bingo in the basement of the United Methodist church 11 years ago where Sally had escaped every Thursday night. She'd never actually gotten a bingo, but had been confident that her new miniature troll doll would be the ticket as a good luck charm.

"Is anybody sittin' here?" Pearl had asked in a husky southern accent, squeezing through the folding chairs, trying not to hit anyone with her bag.

"No," Sally had said in an airy voice, barely looking up from her bingo cards. She'd had twelve cards laid out on a mat in her standard rectangle. The mat had been surrounded by little troll dolls and other suitable luck trinkets she'd collected over the years. Her signature pink dabber had been standing sentinel in the corner, ready for action. She'd lifted her handmade bingo bag from the chair and placed it between her feet. Her apple cheeks had flushed as she'd bent over.

"Nice bag," Pearl had said, looking down at the floral pattern.

"Thank you," Sally had said and smiled. She loved the custom matching bag, mat, and seat cushion she had sewn. She had considered trying to make money from selling them, but Harold had reminded her that it wasn't a practical use of her time. Harold had done that a lot.

She'd watched Pearl unzip a brown beat-up leather pouch, pulling out various dabbers and her tchotchkes. "Have you ever been here before?" Sally had asked, pushing her glasses up on her nose.

"Nope. I usually go over to the Baptist church, but their bingo callers got food poisonin' from the sloppy joes last week, so they had to cancel." Pearl had carefully arranged her ring of good luck charms in front of her while she'd talked.

"Oh, my," Sally had said. She'd always brought snacks from home but sometimes splurged on a Coke and candy bar.

"I'm glad I don't like sloppy joes, or I would've been sick with 'em. If you ask me, Marion got 'em sick on purpose for revenge. She hasn't got a bingo in months and is bitter about it. She yaps about it all the time." Pearl had surveyed her bingo card layout. Then she'd plucked up a rubber ducky and switched it with a yellow ceramic turtle.

Sally had gaped. "You think she would poison people?"

Pearl had stood, putting her hands on her hips, and nodded. "Marion's got a reputation for pitchin' a hissy fit with a tail on it. And you know what, you can't trust people. You gotta keep your eye on them all the time."

Sally had tipped her head and contemplated. Then she'd said, "Maybe. But I think people are basically good."

A tall man in cowboy boots with a handlebar mustache had announced in a deep voice through the crackly microphone, "This is your fifteen-minute warning."

Sally had pulled up her sleeve to double-check the time on her watch.

Pearl had ignored him and continued. "Not me," she'd said, shaking her head. "Guilty until proven innocent in my book. Some people say that's harsh, but I don't care. I've read too many of those true crime stories. People are crazy and will do all kinds of awful things."

Sally had pulled her wallet out of her bag and said, "I'm going to grab a pop. Would you like anything?"

"Can you grab me a Coke?" Pearl had asked, digging through her purse for a dollar.

"Don't worry about it. I'll be right back." Sally had smiled at Pearl. She'd liked the spunky woman, thinking that maybe they could become friends.

During intermission, Sally had asked, "Are you married?"

"Widow. My Johnny and I were married for 21 years. I miss the old fool, but what're you gonna do?"

Sally hadn't been sure what she thought about that. She hadn't wanted Harold dead, but if he'd disappeared one day, she wouldn't have been devastated. Her stomach had flipped with guilt, and she'd looked down at her folded hands. Pearl had sat down with a satisfied breath. "What about you, kid? You married?"

"Yes," Sally had said, twisting her ring around her finger. "His name is Harold. We have three children."

"Oh, well, that's nice. Children are a blessin'."

Before Sally could have commented, the microphone had squeaked loudly, making everyone jump, gasp, and then laugh. The caller's booming voice had announced, "First number, B - four."

5

Plaid Recliner

That night Sally warmed up one of the casseroles dropped off by a neighbor and ate at the kitchen table. The casserole needed salt, but she didn't feel like getting up to grab it. Sally wasn't even hungry. People had been so kind to make food for her. *I'm obligated to try to at least eat some of it,* she thought as she picked at the tuna noodle casserole.

Pearl had made a strong case for a trip to Mexico, painting a picture of palm trees and umbrella drinks. Sally was torn. She didn't want to disappoint Pearl, but she was not sure she was interested in some big adventure. Besides, what would her kids think? She had responsibilities here. She needed to finalize the headstone. She needed to settle Harold's affairs. A trip would be an impractical use of her time.

After washing the dishes, she settled in Harold's recliner and clicked on the True Crime Network, her favorite station. She also loved true crime books and even watched videos on the internet when Harold was home and hogging the television. When a commercial came on, she muted the sound and leaned back, closing her eyes.

She rubbed her hand along the armrest and thought about her marriage. Her entire life had been spent in the shadow of Harold's temper. He had never hit her; that would have been a clear sign to leave. Instead, he'd hurt her in a million little ways. Who would she have been if she had married someone else? Or not married at all? She let out a shaky breath and reminded herself that he wasn't a monster. He was just unhappy. And he'd made everyone around him unhappy as a result. Had he even known how much damage he'd done over the years?

Amid the storm of emotions, something began to bubble up inside her. Sally's heart started to pound, and she clenched her jaw. This stupid chair. She had tried to get Harold to replace it several times. She'd even bought him a new chair for Christmas, and he had made her return it. Harold had loved this chair more than anything, maybe more than he'd loved her.

She clenched her fists and pushed herself out of the chair, whipping around to look at it. The plaid fabric was fraying and faded with age.

It was ugly. It was too big for the room. And it smelled.

She was overcome with the compulsion to get the chair out of the house. She leaned her shoulder into the chair and pushed it towards the front door. She grunted and struggled against the Berber carpet, but the legs kept catching.

There had to be a better way. She pushed the chair over onto its side with a *humph*. The cushion somersaulted across the living room and landed near the fireplace. She turned the chair a few times, trying to figure out how she would get it through the door. Beads of sweat broke across her forehead, and she wiped them away with the back of her hand.

She pulled open the door and stepped back.

The curb. That is where this stupid chair belonged. That was the destination for this hideous piece of furniture. She grabbed a cloth measuring tape out of her sewing box and measured the width of the door frame and the chair. It wasn't going to fit.

Sally screamed in frustration and then stomped through the kitchen to the garage, pulled Harold's old metal toolbox off the shelf, and grabbed the hammer. She swung it gently as she walked back to the living room. The weight felt good in her hand. She was going to enjoy this.

She stalked up to the chair and swung the hammer. The padding muted the sound of the hammer hitting the stubborn wood as she worked to separate the back of the chair. With each swing of the hammer, she rejoiced in the destruction. After a few swings, she realized the recliner wouldn't give up easily. Her breath heaved as she weighed her options.

Damn him. Damn him for being a crappy husband, and damn him for dying. She swung the hammer repeatedly, finally letting out a frustrated scream as the wood gave way. Her neighbors would probably think she'd gone mad as she dragged the two pieces of the chair out to the curb. The trash truck wouldn't come for two days, but she didn't care.

Rich brown soil marked the grooves in the bright green grass trailing behind the recliner's frame. The grass was damp from the automatic sprinklers, making the journey to the curb easier. Two trips, and she was satisfied. She brushed her sweaty hands on her jeans and turned away from the chair. Long shadows from the tree-lined street followed her back to the house. Fireflies were starting their nightly dance. She rolled her shoulders and sniffed. The world was still turning, and life continued.

Letting the storm door slam behind her, she scanned the living room. It seemed bigger and brighter. It still needed some fresh paint, but this was a good start. With a satisfied smile, Sally went to the fridge and pulled out one of Harold's beers. She cracked it open and took a long drink. Maybe she would go to Mexico.

6

Ten Years

Sally headed into her bedroom and set the beer down on her nightstand, part of a matching set. The wood creaked as she slid open the drawer where she kept the important papers for the family, like birth certificates, life insurance, that kind of thing. In the middle of the stack, she removed an oversized envelope. Sitting on the side of the bed, she unclasped the flap and opened it. Reaching inside, she pulled out her passport. She set the envelope next to her on the bed and held the passport in both hands. She ran her fingers over the gold embossed lettering and opened it. She hadn't looked at it in years.

A black and white version of Sally's face stared back at her. Her hair was shorter, and her face had less age on it. But her eyes twinkled with the expectation of adventure. That had been a good day. She smiled at herself.

Her smile faded as she flipped through the rest of the blue pages. Aside from the ornate backgrounds, they were empty. Not one stamp had been placed inside. Scanning the dates, she sucked in a breath. The passport was only good for one more year. How had so much time passed?

She thought about how excited she had been to go on an anniversary trip to Paris, London, or Jamaica. She hadn't cared. She'd just wanted to experience the world. Harold hadn't exactly agreed to go when she'd first brought it up, but he hadn't refused either. So she had been planning, just in case.

And one night, she had spent extra time getting her hair and makeup just right. She'd changed into a new dress in his favorite color. She had made his favorite meal, meatloaf and mashed potatoes, lit some candles, and had even had a cold beer cracked open for him when he came home. If he'd suspected anything, he hadn't let on. She'd watched the clock tick as they ate, waiting for the right moment. Midway through the meal, she had broached the subject again.

"I have been doing some more research about our anniversary trip," she had said in a lilting voice.

Harold had been focused on the baseball game on television in the living room. "Hmm."

Sally would not be deterred. She'd cleared her throat and continued, "And I think we should go to Paris. September is a beautiful time to go."

Harold had gotten up to grab another beer. "Go where?"

"To Paris. Remember, we talked about going for our anniversary this year."

Pulling the tab on the beer can, he'd raised his eyebrows. "You must be talking about you and your new husband." He'd shaken his head and slid back into his seat.

"But wouldn't it be fun? You deserve a vacation for how hard you work."

Harold had stabbed at the peas rolling around on his plate. "Maybe, but I am not going to Paris."

Sally's chest had tightened. Her mouth had gone dry. She'd set her wrist down on the table, still holding her fork. "Why?"

"Why what?" He'd asked, gnashing on a mouthful of food.

"If you don't want to go to Paris, we could go somewhere else."

The sound of his fork clattering to his plate had made Sally jump. He'd looked at her. "I don't know why you thought this was a good idea. It's a waste of money and time."

Sally's heart had deflated. She'd blinked back tears as Harold had kept talking.

"You should know this. Who would watch the house? And what if the kids need you? You can't just abandon your children."

"The children are grown."

"You're still their mother." Harold had picked up his fork and started eating again.

Sally's appetite had been gone. But Harold would have noticed if she didn't eat, and she hadn't wanted to fight, so she'd picked at her food. It had been bad enough her dream trip had been shot down. She hadn't wanted to get yelled at, too.

The trill of the phone drew her back to the present. She set the passport on her dresser, put the envelope back into the nightstand, and closed the drawer. She grabbed her beer and made her way to the living room to see who was calling, Mexico on her mind.

7

Kidnapped or Something

Tuesday, June 21st

Sally watched Lauren climb out of her blue minivan and walk past the broken recliner on the curb. Lauren paused, raised her sunglasses, and examined the plaid carcass. Then she shook her head and walked towards the house. She stopped once and turned to look at the chair again.

As she reached the steps, she said, "I see you got in a fight with the recliner." Her tone hid a mischievous laugh.

"Yes, and I won." Sally smiled and folded her into a hug. When Lauren pulled back, she met Sally's eyes.

"Seriously, are you okay, Mom? Your doctor could prescribe some anti-depressants. All you have to do is ask. I don't want to see you on an episode of *Snapped*."

"Oh honey, sometimes life is just sad, and you have to feel the pain. Are you okay?"

"No, but I will be. Now, what's this about a trip?"

Sally smiled and grabbed her arm, pulling her towards the bedroom.

Twenty minutes later, Sally pulled a white t-shirt out of the blue plastic tub next to her feet. She shook it out for inspection. "Shoot; there's a stain." She wadded it up and threw it into the corner.

She had dragged the tub out of her closet and added it to the similar tubs scattered around the room, all open and overflowing with clothing. She had no idea what to pack for two weeks in Mexico.

Lauren sat on the bed with a leg tucked under her and watched. "Are you sure you should be going to Mexico right now? Dad just passed away, and it's not safe down there."

Sally knew her daughter had been talking to Joel again. Joel didn't understand and just filled Lauren's head with stories. Sure, Sally didn't travel. She had been a homebody when the kids were growing up, and Joel thought her head would end up on a pike. But he was wrong. Sally had always secretly wanted to travel, but after years of begging and arguing, she had just given up.

Sally shook her head. "I'm going with Pearl; I'll be fine. Stop talking to Joel." She wasn't sure she believed it, but she was sick of everyone telling her what she should or shouldn't be doing. She continued sorting outfits into piles on the bed.

"He made some good points, Mom. How well do you know her?"

"She's been my friend for years," Sally said, holding a floral blouse in front of her and biting her lip. "You met her that one time at bingo, remember?"

"For your birthday?"

"Yes, I think it was three years ago. She sat next to me on the other side."

Lauren tapped her chin, thinking. "I remember her. Southern accent, big blue eyes, chin-length white hair?" She looked to Sally for confirmation. After Sally nodded, she continued. "Did she even come to dad's funeral? If she did, I didn't see her there." Lauren narrowed her eyes.

Sally dropped the shirt on the bed. "She didn't know your father. She was my friend, not his. I think you'd like her. She's good for me." Sally didn't have many friends and rarely brought them around the house. If she did, Harold would pretend to be friendly and then get angry later about something silly. It wasn't worth it.

"Are her husband and kids giving her grief about going?"

"She is a widow, and I don't think she ever had kids." Sally tipped her head and tried to remember if she ever talked about kids. How did she not know such important information about her best friend? Probably because she never wanted to talk about her family, and whenever Sally brought it up, she always changed the subject.

Lauren reached into the pile on the bed and pulled out a pair of shorts, handing it to Sally to consider. "You know, those bingo ladies can get pretty wild. Rumor is they go to bingo and then head down to the VFW to drink and dance on tables. She's not going take you and get you arrested, is she?" Lauren was smiling.

Sally didn't pick up on the levity. Instead, she grabbed another pair of shorts and held it up to her waist before throwing it into a growing pile in the corner of her room. "Can you imagine anything that I could do to get arrested? Goodness, no. We're just going to have a quiet time on the beach at an adults-only resort."

Lauren raised her eyebrows. "Adults-only? Are you sure it isn't a nudist resort?"

Sally paused; she wasn't sure. It wasn't out of the realm of possibility that Pearl would book a vacation at a nudist resort either by accident or on purpose. "Of course," she said with confidence that she didn't feel. "It's a perfectly respectable place and it's going to be a lovely time." She pulled the lid off another tub and started looking through bathing suits.

Lauren picked at a piece of lint on the quilt. "Don't you need a passport?"

"I have one." Sally held up a bathing suit, and when Lauren wrinkled her nose and shook her head, Sally threw it in the corner. "And it expires in a year, so I need to use it." Sally had never been out of the country. She hadn't even been on a plane for twenty years. Harold had hated flying and he'd insisted on driving on the few vacations they took.

Lauren grabbed a pillow and hugged it to herself. Then sighed in resignation. "All right, Mom, I hope you're careful. I don't want you getting sick or kidnapped or something worse."

"Really, Lauren. I've watched enough crime drama to avoid any real danger."

"I don't know. What if you get asked to be a drug mule, get arrested at the border, and spend fifteen years in a Mexican prison?"

"Oh, stop. That doesn't even happen unless you leave the resort." Sally had seen several stories about unfortunate tourists who ventured from their hotel and disappeared. That wouldn't be her.

"Yes, it does, and you know it."

Sally pursed her lips. "I think I'm smart enough to avoid being a drug mule."

"Just promise me you'll be careful."

"Pearl has everything planned out. The resort is in Playa del

30

Carmen, a tourist area. It will be fine. Now help me pick out some things to take. What do people wear in Mexico, anyway?" She picked up a sequined pink bomber jacket and held it up in front of her torso.

Lauren wrinkled her nose. "You will get arrested by the fashion police, if nothing else."

The doorbell rang, and Pearl's voice echoed down the hall. "Yew-hew, anybody home?"

"We're in the bedroom," Sally called back.

Pearl appeared in the doorway and dramatically put her hand over her heart, "Thank the baby Jesus, you're alive."

"Why wouldn't I be?" Sally asked, pushing the top down on a pale blue tub.

"Have you seen your front yard? Someone murdered that poor defenseless Barcalounger. Had no idea what I'd be walkin' into. Half expected some horror scene. I was fixin' to call the police just in case."

Lauren stifled a laugh with the back of her hand.

Sally frowned. "I am fine. I just decided to get rid of that old chair, and it wouldn't fit through the door, is all."

"That's like sayin' cuttin' up banana bread with a chainsaw is a perfectly reasonable way to slice toast."

"Oh, stop," Sally said, "it isn't that bad."

Pearl shook her head and asked Lauren, "Has your mama lost her marbles?"

Lauren chuckled, "I don't think so," then she turned to Sally. "I'm glad you got rid of that chair. It was hideous."

"Well, I agree with you on that point for sure." Pearl surveyed the room. "Looks like a tornado went through here. Whatcha doin'?"

"Oh, I just figured I would go through some of my old things and see if anything was Mexico-appropriate."

Pearl narrowed her eyes, "This old stuff won't do," she said, picking up a pair of jean shorts and dropping them onto the bed. "You don't gotta be wearin' stinky cast-offs from those uppity women across town. Let's get you some new stuff. You won't even have to hide the shoppin' bags when you get home." She winked.

Sally flinched and looked at Lauren, who was looking at the bed. Pearl realized her mistake. "Oh shoot, I didn't mean nothin' by it. Just thought you might wanna get a few new things for our trip."

Sally didn't know what to say. Luckily, Lauren sighed and said, "She's right, Mom. No one is holding you back anymore. If you want to go shopping, go."

"Oh, I don't know," Sally said.

Pearl sat on the edge of the bed. "I adore you, Sally, but if I had a dollar for every time, you said that, I'd be a rich woman sippin' tea under a magnolia tree."

Lauren smiled and nodded. "She has always said that. But it's a ruse because anyone who knows my mom knows that if she wants something bad enough, she will figure out a way to get it."

"Now stop it," Sally said, unsure whether or not to be offended. "I don't need the two of you ganging up on me."

"Fair enough. Hey, did I tell you I am considerin' puttin' my house up for sale?" Pearl lived in a rambling old house downtown. The town doctor built it in 1917, and Pearl's husband had surprised her with it fifteen years ago. He had always wanted to live in a historic home, so he'd carried her over the threshold of their dream house, and they'd set out to restore it.

Sally paused and pulled at the hem of her shirt. "What do you mean?"

"Oh, I just don't need that big house anymore and-"

Sally cut her off. "You can't move away."

Pearl tucked her chin into her neck. "Oh, my stars, calm down. I ain't movin' away, just into a smaller place."

Sally's eyes welled with tears, and she looked away. "I don't think I can handle any more changes."

"Oh honey, now let's not go cryin'. You can't get rid of me that easy." Pearl surveyed the room, "Heck, maybe I'll just park myself here and stay for awhile."

"Maybe you can talk her into getting rid of some of these clothes," Lauren added.

Sally sniffed. "It might be nice to have a roommate."

Pearl patted her head, "No more cryin'. We got some shoppin' to do."

8

Where the Wind Goes

The next few weeks were a blur for Sally. Her pastor suggested she join a grief support group at church, so she did. Henry suggested she sell her car and drive Harold's, which was newer, so she did. Pearl brought over paint samples and suggested they paint the living room, so they did. Slowly the numbness began to wear off. Sally even smiled one morning in her sunflower kitchen, looking out the window, watching a hummingbird flutter above her feeder.

She decided to learn some Spanish. Sally downloaded a language learning app on her phone at her son Henry's suggestion. Using the headphones she got for her last birthday, she worked through the first few lessons reasonably quickly. She was proud of her progress but admitted, if only to herself, that learning Spanish was much more challenging than she thought it would be.

When she asked Pearl if she wanted to practice, Pearl laughed and said, "We only need three words for the trip, *banõ*, *dinero*, and *hola*. And that last one's just bein' polite."

Sally ignored her and plowed ahead with her lessons. But after a few days of figuring out why verbs needed to be masculine or feminine, Sally settled for knowing the short list of words and phrases she had picked up, and quit.

The weeks changed the pain of losing Harold from a crushing blow to a dull ache that she sometimes forgot was there. As much as she grieved all the changes in her life, she started to revel in her newfound freedom. She stayed up, slept in, and ate what she wanted. While her kitchen was back to being spotless, she hadn't cooked a full meal since Harold died. She had never loved cooking, and now she didn't need to. It was liberating.

She and Pearl spent hours combing the sale racks at the local mall and, at Sally's insistence, digging through piles of clothing at the Methodist church bag sale. They found some beautiful resort clothing that must have been donated by one of the rich women from the west side of town.

There were still moments, sometimes in the middle of the night or standing in the local grocery store cereal aisle, when Sally felt a sudden wave of grief crashing down around her. Then came the self-doubt and guilt. Last week she'd had to sit down and lean against the boxes of corn flakes to catch her breath. A young woman in a blue vest had rushed over to see if she had fallen, which had made it worse. She had scrambled to her feet and brushed off the attempts for assistance. She'd been sad, not broken.

The guilt lingered. Sally had been a good wife and mother, but every time she smiled or found herself daydreaming about Mexico, it felt like a betrayal.

"Maybe I shouldn't go," she said to Lauren, who stopped by after work to drop off a book she had borrowed. "Your brother has been sending daily articles about crime and water contamination. He is dead set against me going."

"Don't be silly. You have to go. You need this, Mom."

"Oh, I don't know. Joel went on and on about how dangerous it was with all the drug cartels. They kidnap Americans and put their heads on pikes."

"Joel is being a jerk. Are you planning on getting mixed up with a drug cartel or hanging out in dangerous places?"

"Of course not."

Lauren took Sally's hand. "Then relax. Just stay at the resort, and you will be fine. Oh, I almost forgot, I got you a little present." She reached into her purse and pulled out a black luggage tag. Sally smiled and eagerly accepted the gift. It said *Where the Wind Goes, I Go* in shocking pink letters, framed by teal flowers on a black background.

Sally's eyes stung, and she hugged her daughter. "Thank you."

When she pulled back, there were tears in Lauren's eyes. "I am so proud of you, Mom." Lauren had always been strong. She used to get frustrated with Sally, demanding to know how she could put up with Harold's attitude and why she didn't just leave him.

"Aw, thank you, sweetie. I am a little nervous about this whole trip." Sally had considered more than a few times that she should cancel. It was impractical. It was irresponsible. She truly was nervous, but it was also the most exciting thing she had ever thought about doing.

Lauren nodded, smiled, and wiped away a tear. "It will be great. I'm sad dad never got the chance to travel like this. Maybe it would have made him easier to live with."

Sally touched her arm. "You know your dad; he hated to travel. I could hardly get him to a restaurant, let alone out of the country."

Lauren wiped her eyes, choked on a laugh, and smiled. "You are going to have so much fun, Mom. I'm a little jealous."

That evening Sally dragged the tubs from her bedroom to the guest room. It was the first time she'd put all the tubs in one place, and even she knew it was a bit excessive. How was she ever going to narrow her clothing down to one suitcase? Her top choices were piled all over the bed, and her new, bright pink, hard-sided bag sat in the middle, empty. Sally carefully laid out her favorite yellow dress across the pillows. Twenty pairs of shoes lined the wall, waiting to be chosen. Sally had packed and unpacked her suitcase six times. She wanted to be sure to bring everything she might need for this adventure. The problem was not being quite sure what the experience might entail.

Sally picked up the luggage tag and ran her fingers over the smooth leather. It was such a thoughtful gift. Lauren had always been kind. She reached across the bed, lifted the empty suitcase over the clothing and onto the floor, attached the tag, and smiled.

9

Come Fly Away

Wednesday, October 13th

Sally pursed her lips and paced the living room. It was almost seven. They were going to be late. She had woken up at 4:00 am and couldn't get back to sleep. Hopefully, she hadn't bothered her neighbors with her early morning vacuuming. But she was so restless and excited that she'd had the energy to burn. She had dusted her blinds, vacuumed the entire house, and wiped down the kitchen again. It would be nice to come home to a clean house.

But, to her surprise, Pearl tore into the driveway in her bright yellow convertible at 7:00 sharp. She slammed the brakes, a plastic daisy stem dancing on the dashboard. Sally shook her head. *I'm glad we aren't driving to Mexico*, she thought.

"Mornin'," Pearl called out, smiling as she walked to the back of the car to pop the trunk.

Sally shivered as she stepped onto the porch. She wasn't sure what to wear for travel, so she'd opted for layers in case the plane was chilly. Even though her breath billowed before her as she talked, Pearl was in a sundress and sandals, utterly unbothered by the cold. As Pearl took Sally's suitcase from her to load into the car, she noticed Sally's raised brows and eyes scanning her outfit. "What? Dress for where you're goin', not where you been."

And with that, she turned on her heel and dragged the suitcase to the trunk, heaving it in with a grunt. Sally just shook her head again. She pulled open the car door, and her stomach did a flip. They were actually doing this. They were going to another country all by themselves. She had to cover her mouth to stifle a giggle.

They eased onto the freeway, and as Pearl prattled on, Sally leaned back and closed her eyes. She hadn't slept well last night. She'd kept tossing and turning and could have sworn she heard Harold snoring at one point. She didn't believe in ghosts, but she had also reached over and turned on the bedside lamp before going back to sleep, just in case she was wrong.

It wasn't until the car stopped and the engine turned off that Sally's eyes fluttered open. They were in a parking garage, dim despite the early morning sun.

"Rise and shine, butterfly," Pearl said, removing her seat belt and kicking open her door.

Sally wiped her eyes and tried to orient herself. She sniffed, which led to a yawn. Pearl was already popping open the trunk as Sally opened the passenger door. Wheeled luggage in tow, they entered the airport through automatic sliding glass doors.

It was early, yet the airport was bustling with travelers. A travel-weary mother bounced a baby wrapped against her chest, standing next to a stack of luggage outside the bathroom. Business travelers took long, purposeful strides, travel backpacks or briefcases in tow.

Sally gaped at the scope of the airport terminal. Her eyes darted around at the people, security, and flashing signs. "Things have changed since the last time I traveled," she said, following Pearl onto the moving walkway and pushing herself to the side for walkers.

Spaced out between the expansive windows were modern sculptures and mixed-media pieces standing sentinel over all of the comings and goings. Sally's eyes twinkled with girlish delight at finding this hidden world. She had traveled so little that even if they turned around and went home now, she would still be grateful for the adventure.

"We should get some breakfast. I could eat the north end of a south-bound polecat, and plane food ain't edible," Pearl said as they passed a row of restaurants and shops.

"Oh, I don't know. Isn't it expensive? Besides, I brought an apple," Sally said, digging around in her bag for the Granny Smith.

Pearl batted her hand away, "Hogwash. We're gettin' a real breakfast. We need to carb load for our trip."

Carb load? What did she think they were going to be doing in Mexico? Sally planned to lay on the beach and read.

"Let's check out the gate and find some grub," Pearl said, stepping off the moving walkway. She stopped in front of the digital screens and pointed at their flight. "A23." She turned to walk and then spun around, "You comin'?"

Sally was still trying to find their flight on the board but relented and followed Pearl, dragging her carry-on behind her. Her eyes darted as they walked, and her heart fluttered at the thrill of traveling out of the country. She absently patted her coat pocket, reassured at feeling the rectangle outline of her passport holder.

Sally's eyes widened when she saw a drug-sniffing German shepherd walking casually alongside its handler, weaving through the passengers. She had seen this on television, but it was jarring to witness the real thing. Seeing the dog catch a scent and the police throw someone down would really be something. Sally followed the dog, turning the top half of her body until she risked falling over. She swallowed a chuckle at herself and turned her attention back to Pearl.

Pearl found her stride and charged down the terminal towards A23. Sally struggled to keep up, and irritation pricked her skin as her eyes were pulled in different directions. They were here with plenty of time to spare. Why couldn't she slow down? Watching the numbers tick down as she followed Pearl, she let out a breath when she saw their gate. Pearl reached it first. She stopped abruptly, checked the board near the gate desk, then turned around. "Okay. Let's eat."

"Wait, isn't there something we need to do, like check in?" Sally couldn't understand why they came all the way down to the gate just to turn around.

Pearl paused, considering. Then she said, using exaggerated gestures, "Who knows? Just somethin' you do. Park your car, go through security, find your gate." She looked back to the gate and then to Sally. "Anyhow, now we know where it is."

Sally pursed her lips. She still didn't understand the rationale but wasn't going to argue about it. She turned and followed Pearl back down the terminal towards the food court.

"This place looks good," Pearl said, waiting to flag down a harried waitress carrying several plates of eggs. The diner had just opened so they could get a booth quickly. Sally needed coffee, and they both ordered the breakfast special. Forty-five minutes later, they gathered their things and headed back down the terminal towards their gate, pulling their carry-on suitcases behind them.

"Got a surprise for you," Pearl said with a sideways glance.

"Really? Not sure I can handle any more surprises."

"Too late. And you can thank your daughter for this one."

Sally's mouth dropped open. Lauren? When had she and Pearl become friends? What in the world had she done? "Are you going to tell me?" Sally asked.

"Hold your horses," she smiled. "Not long now."

Sally frowned. She hated surprises. All this traveling was surprising enough without whatever they had concocted.

They arrived at the terminal and took two seats near the window. A beleaguered young mom leaned forward with her elbows on her knees, watching her toddler smear the windows with his fingertips and pointing as planes taxied about the runway. Sally tugged on the hem of her jacket. She glanced at her watch. Their flight was supposed to take off in half an hour. Why weren't they boarding yet? Maybe they would be late. What about their transport to the resort? Perhaps they would miss that and be stuck in the airport. This was a bad idea.

"C'mon," Pearl said, patting her knee.

"What?" Sally said.

"Time to board," Pearl stood up and grabbed her suitcase.

Sally stood and looked around. No one else was moving. "Are you sure?"

"Oh, my stars. 'Course I'm sure."

Sally followed Pearl up to the door to the gangway and laid her boarding pass down on the scanner. It beeped, and she stepped forward. Sally imitated what Pearl had done, and when she heard the beep of approval, a satisfied smile spread across her face.

Her wheeled suitcase hummed as it traveled down the ramp to the plane. She looked at her boarding pass, confirming her seat, 2B. That would be nice. It was close to the front so they could get off the plane quickly.

When Pearl stopped in the second row and slid into the oversize first-class seats, Sally froze.

"Surprise," Pearl said, flashing jazz hands.

"How did you...?" Sally asked, glancing behind her, then scooting into the seat to let people pass.

"Lauren used her points to upgrade us. Ain't it somethin'? I wonder if they serve tequila this early in the mornin'."

Sally beamed as she ran her hand across the smooth leather armrest. This was too much. She had hardly flown, and had never traveled first class anything. She would need to pay Lauren back whatever the extra charge was.

"You're grinnin' like a possum eatin' a sweet tater," Pearl said.

"I have no idea what that means, but this is so nice. It's too much."

"Nonsense," Pearl said, waving her off. "Let's get some champagne." When she saw Sally's disapproving look, she said, "What? They can add some orange juice to yours if you want." Then she reached up and hit the call button, still grinning like a Cheshire cat.

10

Welcome to Nueva Vida Del Mar

After traveling on a two-lane highway about an hour south of the airport, they finally turned onto a narrow drive bordered by palm trees and bushes on each side. The road meandered towards the resort, opening up to a circle drive with a fountain in the center. A white two-story stucco building with a red tiled roof peeked through the trees. A cobblestone path led to an arched entrance with iron gates swung wide on either side.

Sally slid open the door of the resort van and stepped out. A blast of heat took her breath away, "Oh my, it sure is hot down here," she said, licking her dry lips. Hopefully, they had bottled water in the room. She had read that you should only drink bottled water in Mexico, or risk being stuck in the bathroom the entire trip.

Pearl followed, sliding to the edge of the bench seat and grabbing the van door for balance, ready to jump down onto the pavement. The driver waved frantically for her to wait and bolted around to the front of the van. He took her hand and helped her down. She thanked him and joined Sally, putting her hands on her hips and stretching her back. "I'm sweatin' more than a hooker in church. But it feels good to have my bones warm." She smiled and smacked Sally on the back.

The resort was just as tropical as Sally had imagined. Lush green bushes with lovely pink flowers flanked the white stucco entrance to the lobby. They stood on the curb, waiting for the porter to unload their suitcases onto a cart. Sally squinted her eyes, one hand perched on her head to keep her straw hat from taking flight. "Do you think I brought enough sunscreen? I only bought three bathing suits. Is that enough?"

Pearl pulled out some cash and handed it to the driver, who gave her a toothy, bright white smile in return. Turning back to Sally, she said, "Oh my stars, it'll be fine." The porter walked ahead, and Pearl led Sally, who was gaping at the tropical surroundings. "All you need is a towel, a Margarita, and your toes in the sand."

Pearl leaned in and whispered, "And if you want somethin' else, maybe a little weed, we can ask Charlie Brown. Pretty sure that's a nickname to keep him out of jail. I heard he walks up and down these beaches handin' out packets like candy cigarettes." She winked and elbowed Sally playfully.

Sally gaped. "I don't need any of that. How do you even know who he is?"

"Oh, my neighbor helped me book this trip. She showed me an online travel thingy, and they said to ask for Charlie Brown if you want anythin' of that nature. We also gotta look out for a waitress named Sue. She's the bee's knees."

Ten minutes later, they were in a resort golf cart, speeding through the winding cement pathways, dodging guests coming back from the pool or beach sun-kissed and smiling. Pearl and Sally sat in the backseat, laughing and grabbing the bar whenever they rounded a corner. The stout, curly-haired driver finally jerked to a stop just past the pool in front of a two-story stucco building in earshot of the waves lapping the beach and flashed a smile at them. He hopped out, helped them down, grabbed their bags, and hustled up the stairs to their room. With a smile, a bow, and a five-dollar bill in his pocket, he retreated to his cart and zipped away.

Sally waved the card she had been given at the desk in front of the black sensor next to the pale pink door just like they showed her and was amazed when it turned green. Things had sure changed since the last time she stayed at a hotel. She pulled the handle down and pushed the door open.

A palm leaf bladed fan spun lazily in the center of the sea foam green room. Crisp white duvets covered both fluffy beds. Pulling back the curtains to reveal the bright blue sea, Pearl said, "Now that is a view."

Sally barely heard her. She was mesmerized. It was just like a postcard. Boats dotted the cerulean horizon. White-flowered bushes framed their balcony. Tears pricked her eyes, and she blinked them back, surprised at the surge of emotion. It was more beautiful than she had imagined.

"Hey now, ain't no cryin' in Mexico," Pearl said, crossing the room and pulling Sally into a hug.

Sally chuckled and wiped her eyes. "I don't know why I'm crying. It's just so pretty."

"Well, if you cry every time we see the ocean, this is gonna be a long trip." Pearl pulled back and patted Sally's arms. "Let's get settled and find some food. Bottled water should be in the little fridge if you want some."

Sally nodded. Pearl grabbed two bottles, handing her one. "We don't need you gettin' dehydrated your first day."

After drinking half the bottle, Sally set to unpacking. She

hung up her clothes neatly in the closet while Pearl plunked her suitcase on a little tropical print love seat and rummaged through it, looking for her bathing suit.

"Ah-ha," she said, spotting a strap and pulling out a navy skirted suit. "Come on now, let's get down to the beach. We got at least two hours of sunlight left."

Sally turned from the closet. "Shouldn't we unpack and get a little orientated first?"

Pearl waved her off. "Nah; we'll figure things out as we go. Gonna be fine. Get one of those bathin' suits you brought and throw it on."

Ten minutes later, they were both clad in bathing suits and big, wide-brimmed hats. Across the front of Pearl's hat, stitched in black thread, were the words *I'm on Mexican Time.*

"What does that even mean?" Sally asked, squinting her eyes to read the text.

"Don't know," Pearl quipped as she kicked off her sandals to walk on the sand. "Just thought it was funny."

"It might be considered offensive," Sally said. As much as she loved Pearl, sometimes she was abrasive.

Pearl stopped and waited for Sally to catch up. "If I worried about being offensive, I'd have to stay home. This world's gone soft."

Sally didn't say anything. Pearl wasn't wrong, but Sally wasn't excited about possibly offending an entire country on their first day here.

"Oh, there are some chairs over there." Sally pointed to two wooden beach chairs under a straw-covered cabana. A pink banner that read *Flamingo Singles* flapped between two trees down the beach from the cabana. Sally's heart ached. Technically she was single, but it was strange. Harold was gone. She was alone. She swallowed a lump in her throat.

"Good pick. Let's go unload our stuff and find that waitress, Sue."

They lumbered across the sand, trying to keep their balance while still managing to look somewhat graceful. "Maybe we should just lay down and enjoy the water, and wait for Sue to find us," Pearl said when they got to the chairs.

Sally nodded and stretched out on one of the beach loungers, watching the calm water and enjoying the warm breeze. The lull of the waves tugged her eyes closed.

Two hours later, Sally opened her eyes. The shadows of the resort stretched to the water, and the outside lighting was on. She panicked and flared up out of her chair. Pearl was stretched out, one foot hanging off of her own lounger. Her mouth was wide open, and she was snoring loudly. Sally shook her leg to rouse her.

"What? Where's Sue? You get me a drink?"

"We fell asleep." Sally looked at her watch. "It's almost dark, and dinner has already started."

Pearl didn't seem to hear her. She wiped her eyes and stretched her arms out. "Whew, I needed that." She swung her legs over the side of the chair and started to gather her things. Sally followed along. Pearl was right. Sally had been more tired than she realized and felt refreshed. Her stomach growled, and she hoped the food was good. She didn't want to eat anything weird.

"Maybe we should just skip dinner and start drinkin'," Pearl said, pushing herself to her feet.

11

Sombrero Shopping

Sally and Pearl followed the dimly lit path to the restaurant, consulting their paper map along the way. They had to double back twice, and Sally let out an audible sigh when the course opened onto a courtyard that served as the center of the resort activity. Guests milled about with drinks in their hands, waiting for the 7:30 show to start on a makeshift stage on the grass across from the restaurant. Sally hoped they would provide an activity guide and made a mental note to ask about it at the front desk so she could mark down which of the shows she wanted to see.

After giving them their room number, a pretty young hostess led them to a small linen-covered table in front of a large window. The candlelight glowed on the faces of couples and friend groups who filled the small restaurant. Sally and Pearl ordered Italian, taking the suggestion of their waiter. As they waited for their food, Sally watched resort guests pass by the window, trying to imagine where they were from. Pearl was scrolling through her phone, then sniffed her glass of wine before taking a drink.

A chipper female voice interrupted their space. "Well, don't you two look cute," said the petite blonde with a ruched hot pink dress beside their table, letting her pink-tipped fingers trail along the edge of the linen tablecloth. She looked about their age, but must have had a good plastic surgeon or great genes.

"Thank you," Pearl said in response.

"Is this your first time at the resort?"

Sally and Pearl both nodded.

"Oh, where are my manners? I haven't even introduced myself. I'm Dottie, a regular here. I know just about everybody. If you have any questions, just ask. I know all the secrets." She leaned in and winked.

"They got bingo here?" Pearl asked.

Dottie grinned. "They sure do. Several times a week." She glanced at her phone and then back at Sally and Pearl. "What brings you south?"

"Sally here needed a vacation," Pearl said.

Dottie's eyebrows raised. "Oh?"

"Well, my husband recently passed, and I thought it was time to get out and see a little bit of the world with my friend here." Sally smiled at Pearl, who gave a quick nod.

"So you've never traveled internationally?" Sally shook her head. Dottie seemed to be working something out in her head. She put a finger to her lips and then spoke. "Hey, did you guys do like most of us and over-pack?"

"No, ma'am," Pearl says, "We did carry-on bags only. I don't trust those airline workers to get my bags where they gottta go, and I ain't gonna risk losin' my favorite bathin' suit."

Sally nodded in agreement. It had taken a lot of work to bring *just* carry-on bags, and Sally had been in doubt they'd be able to, but using zip-lock bags and pushing the air out to compress everything seemed to do the trick.

"Huh," Dottie said casually. "Well, good for you girls. How many days are you here for?" She patted her hair with the palms of her hands.

"Nine days," Sally said.

Dottie raised her eyebrows. "Nice." Someone across the room caught her eye, and she waved her hand. Then she turned back to the "girls" and said, "It was nice to meet you both. I am sure I'll see you on the beach. Have a great night." She flashed a bright smile and then paraded across the room, waving to people as she went.

"She seemed nice," Sally said.

Pearl plucked a dinner roll out of the basket on the table. "Nice enough."

"I like the idea that she knows everyone. It's like a family down here." Sally was heartened to think that they'd already made a new friend. And if Dottie knew as much as she said, maybe she could give them some advice about the activities. Sally would make sure to look for her tomorrow.

"After dinner, we should go to the bar," Pearl said.

Sally groaned inwardly. She was tired and just wanted to go to bed.

"I heard that," Pearl said.

Sally leaned back in her chair. "Sorry. Aren't you tired from today?"

"You had a two-hour nap, remember?"

Sally had forgotten. Grief seemed to make her perpetually tired and filled her head with fog. "Right. Okay, one drink. But then I want to unpack and read for a while."

"Deal."

The server appeared and placed two steaming plates of pasta in front of them.

"What do you want to do this week?" Sally asked. "I thought we could stop by the front desk on the way to our room and get a program or something. It would be nice to put together a schedule for the week so we don't miss anything."

Pearl twisted the fettuccine around her fork. "The question is, what *ain't* we gonna do? Time to have some real fun." She had a twinkle in her eyes that Sally was worried would lead to trouble.

After dinner, they walked over to the courtyard. A little market had been set up with local vendors selling jewelry, paintings, and other souvenirs.

"Look at all this great stuff. Let's get sombreros."

"Oh, I don't know."

"Oh my stars, you gotta loosen up."

Pearl made a beeline for the hat rack and plopped a purple sombrero on her head, grinning. "What do you think?"

"You look like a tortilla commercial."

"You're just jealous because I make this look good."

Sally laughed. "That must be it."

Pearl returned the hat to its perch, and they continued to the next table.

Thirty minutes later, Pearl had purchased a small bottle of natural vanilla and a pair of sunglasses. "My dogs are barkin'," she said, looking at her feet.

Sally agreed. Her feet were aching and swollen from travel.

"Come on, let's go watch some TV and put our feet up. We can get up and hit the beach in the mornin'."

Sally was so relieved she could have kissed her.

12

Naming Pelicans

Thursday, October 14th

Sally couldn't contain her smile. After applying sunscreen and packing two paperbacks in her beach bag, they were ready to go.

"Beach or pool?" Pearl asked.

"Oh, I don't know," Sally replied, her hand absently smoothing her hair.

Pearl considered. "It's a bit windy. We got plenty of time for the beach later. Probably best to start with the pool."

The sun warmed Sally's cheeks as they walked through the peaceful resort. Most guests were still in bed or wandering, bleary-eyed, in search of coffee.

Sally laid her towel out on the poolside chaise and slipped a tube of sunblock out of her straw bag. At breakfast, they had run into a woman with a horrible sunburn. She'd looked like an overcooked lobster, and Sally did not want to make that mistake.

"Didn't you just do that back in the room?" Pearl asked,

watching her squeeze a line of the white lotion onto her arm.

"Yes, but I don't want to get sunburned. The sun here is so strong. You saw that woman at breakfast."

Pearl slapped her floppy hat on her head and said, "I'm goin' to the bar for a drink. You want one?"

Sally stared. "It's nine in the morning."

"Yup, and the bar just opened. What do you want?"

Sally slathered up her legs. "Oh, I don't know. I've never had a drink this early."

Pearl clucked her tongue. "I'll get you a breakfast drink. How 'bout that?"

Pearl came back ten minutes later, holding two Bloody Marys, each with a skewer of pickles and olives six inches high. "Here you go, breakfast in a glass."

By mid-morning, the sun was blazing, and a cannonball contest had started among a group of young men. Sally and Pearl decided to head to the beach to enjoy the light breeze still blowing in from the water. Sally could feel eyes on them as they gathered their things. They had prime lounge chairs that were about to be up for grabs. Several people were eyeing their progress.

Pearl leaned over and whispered, "Maybe we should hold an auction and make some money off these chairs."

Sure enough, as soon as they were a few steps away from the chairs, an older couple, moving with surprising speed, swooped in to claim them, leaving at least two sets of disappointed onlookers in the dust. *Good for them*, Sally thought.

An hour later, Sally and Pearl stood waist-deep in the crystal blue ocean water, their floppy hats waving in the slight breeze. They watched little fish swim around them. Seagulls patrolled the air, looking for easy prey or leftover food on the beach.

Pelicans sat on the rocks of the jetties that reached out like fingers every third of a mile on the beach, dividing the resort and providing protection from rip currents.

Pearl watched the pelicans leave and return to the same spot. She pointed to one and said, "See that one? That stupid one? His name is Elmer Fudd. He was sittin' there and just plumb fell over, no reason whatsoever. And that one, over there? He's smart, see, watchin' the fish and just waitin' for the right moment to strike. We're gonna call him Albert Einstein. And that over there? That's Martha Stewart. She's guardin' that little spot where the rocks are put together just so."

Sally was laughing at the commentary when a woman waded up beside them.

They looked over simultaneously, and both of their mouths dropped open. A woman with brown permed hair and a rose tattoo on her collarbone stood next to them, topless. She looked to be in her early 40s. She dragged her fingertips through the water and asked earnestly, "How do you know their names?"

Pearl and Sally shared a look. Pearl turned away to hide her disbelief. Sally wasn't sure how to respond. Was she serious? After a beat, it was clear she was. Sally bit her lip and offered, "I thought the same thing. No, she's just naming them as we go. No official names exist, but I see how you'd make that mistake."

The woman just nodded and looked at them quizzically. "I guess that makes sense. Where are you guys from?"

Sally said, "Michigan. What about you?"

"We're from Minnesota. My husband is over there." She pointed to a man sitting on the beach, laughing with a group of people.

"Ah." Sally struggled not to let her eyes fall. Her face was hot, and she could see Pearl from the corner of her eye, struggling not to laugh at Sally's embarrassment over the topless newcomer. "What do you guys do up there?" Sally asked politely.

"We run a nudist resort and a swingers club."

"A what?" Sally said.

Pearl elbowed Sally. "You heard her; they run around nude and *swing.*" With that, Pearl swung her hips in a circle and thrust her elbows backward.

Sally's hand went to her mouth, "Oh my goodness! I didn't know that was a thing anymore."

"It is," the woman said with a smile, "and we love it. We used to come down here to the swinger resorts all the time, but most of them are shut down now. There is the nudist resort, all-inclusive, next door. We probably should've booked there, but we weren't sure about that place, so we came here instead."

"Oh?" said Sally. There was a nudist resort next door? Her daughter was right.

Pearl wrinkled her nose and said, "Y'all allowed to be topless on this beach? With the public and kids down the beach'n all?"

The woman nodded somberly. "I checked. It's perfectly legal to be topless on all public beaches in Mexico."

"Really?" Pearl said, her eyes growing wide.

"It is. I'm Shannon, by the way. And my husband up there? His name is Ricky." She waved and bounced on her feet, trying to catch her husband's attention. "Hey Ricky, say hi to these ladies."

Ricky, thankfully with swim trunks on, stood up and waved, smiling, a cigar hanging out of his mouth. On his head he wore a ballcap that read *Minnesota Twins.*

"Well, it was nice talking to you, Shannon. I'm sure we'll see you around," Sally said.

"I hope so. We're trying to make new friends here and, hopefully, no one's too offended about topless sunbathing, but, you know, the girls love to come out and play, and it's legal, so here I am."

"Hey Shannon! Beer's getting warm," Ricky shouted from the beach. All three women turned to see what he was yelling about. He held up a can of beer in front of him.

Shannon turned, left the water and jogged up the beach, her red bathing suit bottoms riding up her butt crack a little bit. Sally shook her head slightly. "I've never seen a woman nude sunbathing."

"No?" Pearl said, "You gotta travel more. They sunbathe nude all over the world. Americans are all uptight about it, but you'll see boobs hangin' out left and right if you go to Europe."

"Really?" Sally asked.

"Heck yeah. We gotta make that our next trip. There are some beaches I could take you to," she said.

"You're not going to expect *me* to nude sunbathe, are you?"

"Oh, no. I mean, forty years ago, I would've been right there with her, peeled that top off, and let 'em hang. But now, I'd get 'em caught in my bikini bottoms. Nope, can't do that anymore. I'm stuck in my old lady hat and swim dress."

"Well, at least you're stuck in Mexico," Sally said.

"Ain't that the truth." Pearl bumped Sally's arm and grinned at her.

A shrill voice interrupted their conversation. It was Dottie. She was shouting instructions to a group of people dragging beach chairs into a circle. She was tying the Flamingo Singles banner between two posts stuck in the sand.

"That's quite a name," Pearl said, lifting her chin towards the banner.

"It's cute. Maybe they all stand on one leg to meet people?" Sally said, giggling to herself.

"I bet Dottie picked it." Pearl lifted her chin at Dottie, clad in a hot pink bathing suit and black sarong.

Dottie turned around and noticed them. "Hey, ladies!" She gave them an exaggerated wave.

Sally waved back. Pearl followed suit, seeming reluctant.

"Don't be rude," Sally chided.

"I ain't being rude. I just don't feel like wavin' at every Tom, Dick, and Harry who waves at me." She huffed and pulled her hat down over her eyes.

When they were done swimming, Sally fell back onto the chaise. "What should we do this afternoon?"

"I already got somethin' planned, and it's a surprise."

13

You Aren't Serious

"What are we going to do this afternoon?" Sally asked before popping a grape into her mouth. She couldn't stop thinking about the surprise activity. She had seen people parasailing and had no desire to be dragged into the air and dropped to her death in some mishap.

They were seated at a table under an umbrella. A seagull was hopping around on the ground squawking for food. Pearl was dipping french fries topped with cheese into ranch dressing. "Goin' kayakin'," she replied nonchalantly.

Sally swallowed and said, "What? You aren't serious."

"As a heart attack."

"Are you sure you're up for kayaking?" Sally asked Pearl. Sally had been taking daily walks for years to keep her energy and flexibility in check. Well, most of the time, it was to get out of the house after Harold had come home from work. But the energy was a bonus; she was confident she could swim in the open ocean without drowning, even if it scared her.

Pearl pulled her chin into her neck. "Of course I am. I do Jazzercise twice a week at home. Pretty sure I can handle some paddlin'."

Sally raised her eyebrows. "Really?"

"Don't look at me like that. I also took a self-defense class last year at the senior center. Anyone who tries to kidnap us will be in for a bad day."

Sally pictured Pearl doing self-defense against some unsuspecting attacker and burst into laughter.

Pearl stared at her with questions on her face. "What's wrong with you?"

"Nothing," Sally said, waving her hand in front of her. "I am just glad to be here with you, friend." Sally wiped her hands with a napkin. "And I'm not afraid. I just didn't think kayaking was our speed. It seems like a young person's activity."

"Good thing we're young at heart because we gotta be there in fifteen minutes," Pearl said firmly. "I reserved two kayaks for us at eleven o'clock."

"Oh, I don't know."

"Oh, no, you agreed to come to Mexico and do everythin' I suggested, and this is what we're doin'. Stop your worryin'. That little cabana boy over there will help us if we need it."

"What if I tip over? Aren't there sharks out there?"

"Oh darlin', there ain't no sharks out there. Come on." Pearl reached her hand down and pulled Sally to her feet.

Sally was pretty sure there were sharks out there, but shark attacks weren't high on the list of all the scary things she had heard about Mexico. She sighed and followed Pearl to the water's edge, where kayaks waited for them like little red beached whales. The young man wearing a name tag that said *Eddie* looked them over and said, "You sure you want to kayak?"

Pearl straightened her shoulders. "Yeah, honey, that's why we signed up. Now, where are the paddles and life jackets?"

He said, "You okay to go? You swim?" He raised his eyebrows and looked at them both for confirmation.

"Honey. We ain't swimmin'; we're kayakin'. Now can we get a life jacket and a paddle? We only got an hour."

"Okay," he said, sharing a look with the other young man rinsing life jackets in pans of soapy water.

Eddie pulled two life jackets off a string between two posts and handed one to Sally. She slipped it over her shoulders and fixed the two clasps in the front; but then noticed the long string hanging down the back and said, "Well, what am I supposed to do with this? Wrap it over my head or around my waist?"

Eddie came over, awkwardly looked at her, and said, "No. That goes there." He pointed between her legs.

Sally's brows knitted together, and she asked again. "Where does that go?"

"It goes between your legs," he said, "and comes up," and he motioned to show her where to put it. Sally's face turned bright red with embarrassment as she reached down between her legs, grabbed the strap, and pulled it up to buckle it.

Pearl slipped her jacket on, stifled a laugh, and then asked him again, "Now, what am I supposed to do with this?" She winked at Sally, who just rolled her eyes. Then she grinned at the young man helping them.

He tried again to explain to her how to attach the strap.

"Ooooh," she said in an exaggerated acknowledgment of his instructions. "I get it. You wantin' me to pull it between my legs and up? Between my legs and then strap it, huh?" He nodded and then skittered away while she completed her task.

He grabbed two paddles and dragged the two kayaks into the water. He looked at them and said, "I will help, okay?"

"You'd better help; I don't know how to do this," Sally said.

"Okay," he said with a big smile. He motioned for Pearl to come to the side of the kayak and sit down, then swing her legs over. When she did, the kayak tipped and rolled over the other side and into the water, which was only about knee-deep.

"Whoa," Pearl said as she went over. Sally burst out laughing.

Eddie was mortified. "Oh, I'm so sorry! So sorry!"

Pearl pushed herself to her knees and said, "My fault. Please gimme a hand up so I can get this done right." He ran over and helped her up. Then he moved the kayak out into deeper water and they tried it again. This time Pearl managed to get into the kayak with her legs swung on top so she could balance. "Alright, hand me the paddle." Relieved, Eddie handed it to her, and she tried paddling backward and forward. Sally just watched, shaking her head.

Then Eddie came up to her and said, "Your turn? You go?" Sally seriously considered bailing out, but she knew Pearl would never let her live it down, so she nodded and held onto her hat while gingerly lowering herself into the kayak, trying to keep her knees together and her back straight. When seated, she tried to pull her legs together because she didn't want to flash anybody on accident, and the young man furrowed his brows and said, "One leg at a time."

Everyone breathed a sigh of relief once they were both in their kayaks with their paddles on their laps.

"Okay, you go out and don't go past rocks, okay?"

"We're not plannin' on crossin' the sea. We got eight more days here. Come on, Sally." Pearl started paddling, and it became apparent that her life jacket was too big for her body: the side straps stuck up over her ears, and the front was covering up her nose. She started paddling up and down the swim area with Sally behind her.

Pearl looked over to the beach. "Well, lookie there. Ain't that Dottie in the hot pink bathin' suit with that stupid singles group?"

"Don't be mean. I think that singles group looks fun," Sally said.

"Ain't you just comin' out of your shell?" Pearl said with a wicked grin.

"Maybe. I like traveling, and this has been exciting. And I think if there was a group that I could join where I could travel all the time, I'd do it."

They stopped paddling and let the tide pull them out a bit.

"Oh really? You'd need a sugar daddy for that," Pearl said. "Or do you got a fortune hidden somewhere that I don't know about?"

Sally thought for a second. "I don't know. Lauren has been helping me with all that. I may have to get a job."

Pearl stopped paddling and turned around to look at her. Her kayak started tipping, so she quickly looked forward again and spoke loudly. "What're you talkin' about, gettin' a job? You're too old to be gettin' a new job."

When they floated to the swim area's outer border, Pearl dipped her paddle back in the water and turned herself around.

"I know," Sally said, "but I may not have a choice."

"Don't you got investments?"

Sally struggled to keep up. Where did all Pearl's upper body strength come from? She spoke through short breaths. "I don't know. Harold always took care of that. I'm - I - there's a whole folder in Harold's office, and I didn't even feel like looking at it after he died."

Pearl rested her paddle across her lap and looked at Sally, saying gently, "Honey, I can understand that, but let me tell you, we gotta figure it all out. You can't just live off nothin', especially if you wanna travel."

Why did she always have to push? Sally didn't want to talk about money or Harold. All of that would be there when she got home. "I know. I know. I don't want to even think about it right now, okay? It stresses me out so much to talk about it and think about it. We're having a good time. Can we just enjoy our vacation and worry about all that when we get home?"

"Alright, but I'll tell you what, unless somebody planted a money tree in your backyard, we're gonna have to do some serious thinkin'. We can't have you end up homeless. And you can't live with me unless you get rid of 90% of your clothes. They ain't gonna fit, even if I stay in my big old house."

14

Tequila Shots

Sally washed the salt water and sand off and sighed as she stretched her back and shoulders, letting the water run over her. She smiled at herself. Her skin was glowing after her day in the sun. Her arms were a little sore from kayaking, but she felt great. Why had she waited so long to travel? How many more passport stamps would she be able to get? Her smile faded as she thought about her finances. What was she going to do? Become a grocery store greeter? She pushed the thoughts down and started humming a Jimmy Buffett tune to drown the questions nagging her.

After she was dressed in her white capri pants and navy striped top, she joined Pearl at the bathroom counter to apply her makeup.

"I'm gonna teach you how to drink," Pearl said, running a brush through her curly hair.

Sally paused mid-swipe of her lipstick and met Pearl's eyes. "I know how to drink."

Pearl smiled wickedly. "Not like this, you don't."

Sally stared at Pearl in the mirror and said, only half-joking,

"Do you have a drinking problem I should know about?"

Pearl scoffed. "'Course not. But what happens in Mexico stays in Mexico." She winked and elbowed Sally in the side.

"You're going to be the death of me." Sally smiled and went back to finishing her lipstick.

They headed to the Mexican restaurant on the far side of the resort. When Pearl tugged on the door, it didn't open. Sally cupped her hands around her face and pressed against the glass to see inside. Workers were moving about, seemingly unaware of the time. A pretty young waitress noticed her and smiled but made no move to unlock the door. Sally turned and shrugged. The sign on the door indicated that they opened at five. Pearl huffed and then plopped down on a chair at the outside tables. Sally slid a chair out and joined her.

"This is why I ain't ever movin' to Mexico," Pearl said. "If they bother to put a time on the door, they should damn well honor it."

"Oh, relax. We're on vacation, remember."

"I know that. I'm just hungry. They could at least bring out some chips and salsa while we wait."

Sally pulled some hand cream out of her purse and unscrewed the cap. When she looked up, she sucked in a breath. A small group was walking towards them. One of the men let out a hearty, friendly laugh. He was tall, with broad shoulders and blue eyes. A white golf shirt offset his bronzed skin. When he met her eyes and smiled, her breath quickened, and her mouth went dry. She gave him a half-smile back and then looked down at her hand cream, trying to remember why she had pulled it out. The group stopped on the other side of the patio, waiting for dinner.

"I saw that," Pearl leaned over and whispered.

Sally's cheeks heated, and she didn't look up. "I don't know what you're talking about."

"Yes, you do," Pearl smirked and then sat up.

Forty-five minutes after they were supposed to begin serving, a young woman pushed open the door to the restaurant.

"Finally," Pearl grumbled.

The restaurant was decorated with colorful sombreros on the wall and paper lanterns hanging over the room in a zig-zag pattern. The waitress, dressed in a bright red dress with white stitching on the edges, led them to a long table in the middle of the restaurant and pointed for them to sit down.

Sally looked around. What in the world? Why couldn't they have their own smaller table? Before she could ask Pearl about it, the group she had seen earlier was ushered towards them. Sally's breath caught in her throat. The handsome man was looking at her and smiling again. She slid onto the bench next to Pearl and stared at the cactus-shaped saltshaker.

When she looked up, the man was sitting across from her, looking at his menu. She lowered her eyes and tried to read the menu on the table before her, but her eyes kept blurring. She couldn't believe she was feeling nervous around this stranger. She was an old lady and a new widow. She sat straight and forced her eyes to focus on choosing her meal.

An elbow to the ribs startled her, and she looked at Pearl, who was looking back at her. The whole table was staring at her, in fact. A waitress stood next to her waiting to take her order. She cleared her throat and looked up. "Sorry." She rambled out her order and the waitress retreated to the kitchen. Sally wasn't sure where to look. She didn't want to be rude at the crowded table, but wasn't sure what to say. Luckily, Pearl came to the rescue.

"I'm Pearl, and this here's Sally. Nice meetin' ya'll."

"I'm Mike," said the man sitting across from them. His voice was warm and deep. He reached his hand out to shake Sally's. She bit her lip and mumbled a greeting while taking his hand briefly. Even after she let go, her skin tingled in all the places they touched.

The man beside him had extra-white teeth, leathery tan skin, and a gold luxury watch on his wrist. He leaned over the table and grabbed a chip. "I'm Chuck. I work with Dottie running the singles group." He shoved the entire chip into his mouth and winked.

Sally smiled in response, but Pearl ignored him.

Throughout the dinner, Pearl chatted with Mike, asking him all the questions Sally would have asked if she had been able to speak. He was from St. Louis and was a widower. He had retired from the military and now traveled. Like most of the people sitting around the table, he was a member of the Flamingo Singles.

Twenty minutes later, they were standing at the bar. Four shot glasses and four lemons were set out before them with a salt shaker in the middle. Pearl was explaining the art of the tequila shot when Chuck slid onto the bar stool next to them. "Hello ladies, can I get you a drink?" Then he noticed the shots lined up in front of them and raised his eyebrows. "Never mind, you ladies are ready to party."

"Thank you for the offer. Would you like to join us?" Sally asked.

Pearl kicked her foot and set her jaw. Sally ignored her.

Sally felt bad for him. He seemed like a nice man, even with his slightly greasy hair and too-white teeth. He probably didn't have a lot of luck with women. Over dinner, he'd mentioned that he was divorced and had no children. *Perhaps that's why he travels all the time*, Sally thought.

Chuck yanked up the waist of his shorts, which were precariously sitting below his belly. "Nah. I'm meeting up with Dottie and the others at a table." He pointed with his luxury watch-clad wrist to three tables that had been pushed together, the Flamingo Singles banner hanging from a rafter of the pavilion. "Just wanted to grab a drink while I waited." He flagged down the bartender and ordered a scotch on the rocks. They made small talk while he waited. He had owned a few Blockbuster stores in New Jersey but had lost most of his money due to what he referred to as "the man." Now he just traveled and did some consulting work to make ends meet.

"Only thing that could tie me down is Spike." Chuck's eyes clouded.

"Spike?" Pearl asked.

He nodded gravely. "Spike is the best friend I ever had. Want to see a picture?"

"Of course, " Sally said.

Chuck fished his phone out of his pocket and held it up to unlock it. Then he scrolled through his photos, a broad smile spreading across his face. "Here he is." He turned the phone around to show Sally and Pearl a picture of a fluffy Pomeranian, sunglasses balanced on his nose. "Isn't he adorable? We bought those on his birthday. I took him to the pier, and we got ice cream."

"What a cutie," Sally said. "Where is he?"

Chuck's face fell. "My ex-wife has him." He muttered an indistinct name that sounded more like a curse. "We split custody. It breaks my heart each time I have to say goodbye to him. Divorce is so hard on families."

Pearl had the good sense to keep her mouth shut. Poor Chuck looked heartbroken. Sally touched his arm. "I'm so sorry. That's awful."

He nodded and wiped his nose. "Thanks. It's hard sometimes." He took one last look at the photo, sighed, and slipped the phone back into his pocket. He downed the rest of his drink and said, "Alright, ladies, time for me to get back to business. See you later."

After he had swaggered over to the group table at the end of the bar, Sally and Pearl turned their attention back to the shot glasses. "Okay, you ready?" Pearl asked.

Sally sucked in her cheeks and then nodded. Pearl walked them through the steps. "Lick, Salt, Lick, Drink, Suck."

Sally shook her head as she sucked the lemon, her face squished up and eyes shut. Pearl grinned with the lemon wedge between her teeth, and Sally laughed.

"Think his fancy watch is real?" Pearl asked after spitting the lemon rind into her hand and setting it on the counter.

"His watch? Why wouldn't it be?"

Pearl shrugged. "Don't know. Those things are expensive. Seems dumb to wear it on vacation. Might as well put a bullseye on your back."

"Never thought about it that way."

Pearl nodded and lifted her second shot glass. "Ready for another one?"

"I need a minute," Sally replied. She wasn't used to drinking and didn't want to do something foolish.

"Oh hogwash, come on," Pearl said, lifting the saltshaker and dangling it between her fingers.

"You ladies ready for some karaoke?" said a handsome younger worker with a name tag that read *Juan*. He did a cha-

cha step as he passed them and headed to the DJ booth in the corner of the dance floor. Sally remembered seeing him behind the bar earlier that evening.

"What's karaoke?" Pearl asked innocently and winked at Sally.

Juan stopped dead in his tracks and turned around dramatically. "You do not know karaoke?" He lifted her hand to his lips, pretended to kiss it, and then gazed into her eyes. "Karaoke is the ancient art of seduction through song. And you, my dear, will make many men fall in love with you tonight."

Pearl shook off his hand. "You get me up there, and the only things that'll come runnin' are vultures, thinkin' they got a dyin' cat on their hands."

He blinked twice and then turned to Sally, taking her hand. "Perhaps you have the gift of song in your heart." He batted his eyelashes at her.

Sally laughed. Heat flushed her body, and she felt heavy and light simultaneously. She wasn't sure if it was the tequila or Juan. "Maybe," she said, turning her head down and to the side.

Juan stepped back and spun her around. "Then you, my dear, are my diamond for tonight." He spun her around out and bowed before heading over to the booth. Just as he reached his destination, he turned and blew her a kiss.

Sally giggled, and Pearl shook her head, smiling.

15

Betty Booby

"What're you gonna sing?" Pearl asked.

"Oh, I don't know. I might just watch tonight."

"I know you can sing. If you don't put your name in, I'm gonna do it for you."

Sally shrugged her shoulders noncommittally and glanced around. At the Flamingo Singles table, Shannon was sitting on Chuck's lap as he whispered in her ear. Ricky sat across from them, drinking a beer and scrolling through his phone.

As they downed their next shot, the music started. Looking over her shoulder, Sally smiled as Juan sang a popular Neil Diamond song, his thick accent and dance moves giving the song a new twist. Sally started tapping her foot and then bobbing her head. When the crowd joined in during the chorus, she did too, her eyes bright with joy. She clapped her hands together and looked at Pearl, who was also singing along, lost in the music.

As the song ended, the crowd cheered and clapped. "Thank you. Now, who will be our next singer?" Juan looked at Sally and pointed to her. "How about you?"

Sally shook her head and bent over to hide her face in Pearl's shoulder. Pearl shook her off. "You gotta get up there."

A moment later, an older man in white linen pants and a matching button-down bounded up to the mic and whispered something in the DJ's ear. The DJ scooted behind the booth and tapped on his laptop. A familiar song by Frank Sinatra began, and the crowd clapped and cheered.

Pearl elbowed Sally and shouted above the din, "That boy can sing!"

Sally nodded. She swayed with the music and let her voice join the rest of the crowd on the crescendo. She watched closely as the following few singers headed up and checked in. She could do this. She didn't know any of these people, so why should she care what they thought? Her conviction solidified when Shannon stepped up, fully clothed, and attempted to sing an old Madonna song. She couldn't carry a tune in a bucket but didn't seem to notice. She shimmied and wiggled her hips, strutting back and forth across the dance floor. She laughed and sang at the top of her voice. The crowd loved it.

Sally thought about the first time she had sung Karaoke. It had been with Pearl. They had gone to bingo, and Pearl had won $100. She'd wanted to celebrate and had insisted they stop at the bar downtown for a drink.

Sally hadn't been in a bar in twenty years. The last thing she'd needed was the town gossiping about seeing her in a place of ill repute. But Pearl had insisted. The evening had ended in triumph as she'd pulled off a decent rendition of a Reba song, and the bar had erupted in applause. It had been a great night.

If Shannon could get up there, so could Sally. She tugged the hem of her shirt down, cleared her throat, and walked over to the DJ booth.

"Ah, my diamond has decided to shine?" Juan asked.

Sally looked back at Pearl, who smiled and motioned for her to keep going. "Yes, do you have any Shania Twain?"

"Of course." He turned the laptop screen to show a list of options.

Sally pointed at one and said, "That will work. Thank you." Sally turned and immediately returned to the bar before losing her nerve.

"You girls gonna sing?" Shannon asked, walking up to them.

"Sally here is," Pearl said, lifting her chin in Sally's direction.

"Nice. You should hear Chuck sing. He may not look it, but he can croon."

"Really?"

"Oh yeah," she said with a faraway look in her eyes. "He visited our resort last summer, and let's just say he was very popular with the ladies."

"You got karaoke at your nudist resort?" Pearl asked with a grin.

"Of course. Why wouldn't we?"

"And people just sing in the nude?" Sally asked incredulously.

"Sure do. That is the point of a clothing-optional resort." She winked at Sally, then let out a yelp as Chuck walked behind her and whacked her on the butt. She shook her finger at him. "Don't start something you can't finish," she called out after him.

"Won't Ricky be mad if he sees you flirting with Chuck?" Sally asked.

"Mad? No way. Chuck and I are friends, if you know what I mean," Shannon giggled. Shannon continued when Sally just stared, obviously unaware of what she meant. "Chuck is a fantastic kisser, and Ricky likes to watch."

An image passed through Sally's mind, and she shuddered. Pearl elbowed her and leaned over to whisper, "Don't ask questions if you don't want the answer."

"Excuse me, ladies, I think Chuck wants to dance." They followed her line of sight, and sure enough, Chuck was standing on the side of the dance floor, hooking his finger in her direction. She giggled again and sashayed over to him, pushing her ample chest up and into the middle of her low-cut white t-shirt.

When she and Chuck began grinding to an old disco tune, Sally turned to Pearl. "Did she mean that they had sex?"

Pearl nodded.

"And Ricky, her husband, likes to... watch?"

Pearl nodded again, a grin threatening to break across her face at Sally's shocked expression.

"And Ricky doesn't get jealous?"

"I got no idea. This may shock you, but I ain't never been much of a swinger."

Sally was mortified. "I didn't mean, I just thought... oh, I don't know."

Pearl burst out laughing. "You should see your face right now. Oh, my stars."

"Stop. I'm nervous enough as it is."

"I can't wait. It's bound to be better than Betty Booby up there." She pointed to Shannon, now grinding against her husband in the middle of the dance floor.

Sally was in the middle of taking a drink and laughed, spitting Jack and Coke out in a cloud. She was wiping her face with a napkin when Juan called her name. Her mouth went dry, and her throat closed up. Great. How was she going to sing if she could barely breathe? Pearl gave her a shove. "Get on up there."

Sally slid off the bar stool and made her way to the micro-phone, weaving through the tables. She swallowed and tried to slow her breathing. She could do this. She passed by Betty Booby and stifled a laugh. It was hard to believe she was here, a bit drunk and ready to sing in Mexico. The first chords of the song rang out through the speakers. Pearl put her fingers in her mouth and let out a loud whistle. Sally held the microphone in one hand and the cord in the other. She looked at her feet, ensuring the cord wouldn't get tangled and trip her in the middle of her song.

She swallowed hard, wishing she had brought her drink up with her. When the words appeared on the screen, she took a deep breath and started. Within the first few notes, a hush fell over the pavilion. Her face reddened with the heat of all eyes on her. But she concentrated on the electronic lyrics and let her voice rise and fall with the familiar melody.

16

Pearl Punches a Pelican

Friday, October 15th

> Hey, darling, I got up early to go for a walk on the beach. Get yourself up and around and come meet me. I'll get us the best chairs.

Sally smiled at the text message. Pearl was always one step ahead of everybody. Sally stretched her arms above her head and let out a long breath. *Another day in paradise*, she thought. A headache danced around the edges of her vision. Her stomach was protesting the previous night's consumption of tequila. She needed some aspirin and dry toast.

Thirty minutes later, she sat outside the buffet at an umbrella-covered table. After washing down two aspirin with some water, she picked up a slice of toast to spread some butter across it.

"Hey there," Dottie called out, waving a hand at Sally and

heading her way. She wore a pink two-piece suit and a sarong wrapped low on her hips. Sally had to admit that she was in great shape, tan and lean.

Sally smiled and instinctively sucked in her stomach. She liked Dottie. "Good morning," she responded.

"Can I join you?"

Sally nodded, and Dottie dropped her beach bag on the chair across from her and headed into the buffet. Sally finished buttering her toast and added some strawberry jelly. Just as she finished her first slice, Dottie coasted out of the doorway with a plate piled high with fruit.

"I brought some fruit for us to share." She plunked the plate down onto the table and handed Sally one of the forks in her hand. "Don't be shy. There's plenty."

Sally took the fork and swallowed her bite of toast. "Thanks." Dottie was sweet. It was too bad she lived so far away. Maybe she and Pearl should join her club. It would be nice for them to have some new friends. She poked at a piece of pineapple with her fork and smiled as the sweet juice filled her mouth. Fresh fruit was her favorite.

"So, what will you do when you get home?" Dottie asked, popping a piece of watermelon into her mouth.

"What do you mean?" Sally asked, surveying the plate for another piece of fruit.

"Are you planning to go to work? Or did your husband have some nest egg set aside for you?"

Sally paused, a slice of melon stuck on her fork. She wasn't sure why Dottie was asking her something so personal. She didn't want to think about money on this trip. Harold had taken care of the bills. He had retired but still worked part-time at the local hardware store. Had that money kept them afloat?

Her appetite vanished. She set her fork down on her plate, the melon getting coated with toast crumbs. She brushed her hands on her shorts and swallowed. "I haven't thought about it."

Dottie pointed her fork at Sally. "Well, you'd better. When my husband died, I was... unprepared." She shook her head. "I had to find a way to make money quickly."

"What did you do?"

Dottie talked between chewing bites of watermelon. "At first, I worked at a trendy little boutique, but that didn't pay enough. Then I tried to sell clothing at one of those home-based businesses, but you can only sell so many tops to your friends. I came here to visit one year, fell in love with it, and here I am." She spread her arms out.

"Do you make enough money running the singles group to live on?"

Dottie laughed. "God, no. But I have found some other lucrative ways to supplement my income." She stabbed a piece of grapefruit. "They allow me to travel and meet fantastic people like you." She plopped it in her mouth and smiled at Sally.

Sally smiled back. Maybe Dottie could give her some ideas about what to do with her life. They talked for a while about the places Dottie had traveled and what she loved about being on the road.

Dottie looked at her phone, a notification lighting up the screen. "It's Chuck. He wants to meet me in his room. He's been so demanding lately. Apparently, he thinks he runs the group. Like he forgot that I started this group and was nice enough to let him be a member." She shook her head. "I need to go put him in his place," she said, grabbing her bag and throwing it over her shoulder. "Can you be a doll and take care of my dishes for me?"

"Of course," Sally said, nodding.

When Sally finally made it down to the beach, her big, floppy hat held down by one hand and her other hand holding her beach bag, she saw Pearl standing in the water up to her waist, feeding fish pieces of a breakfast roll. Sally dropped her bags on the sand next to the chairs covered in the telltale bright beach towels that Pearl insisted they buy instead of using the hotel's towels "because then we would always know where we were sittin' in case we forgot."

Sally made her way down into the water and was about ankle deep when suddenly, a pelican came out of nowhere from the left side of her vision. It was flying about even with the water, and heading straight towards Pearl. Sally opened her mouth to try and scream, but before she could warn Pearl, the pelican was right on top of her, and Sally watched, horrified, wondering what the bird was going to do to her friend. Pearl's head snapped up from where she was watching the fish just in time to catch the Pelican in her line of sight, and Sally couldn't believe it when Pearl reached a hand up and punched the pelican in the face. It screeched and flew off, and Pearl returned to feeding the fish little pieces of bread like it hadn't happened. Sally shouted, "Pearl, are you okay?"

Pearl turned. "I'm fine – that ain't the first time I punched a pelican. I grew up down south, remember?" Sally wasn't sure what growing up down south had to do with punching pelicans but nodded, and Pearl went back to feeding the fish.

Remind me never to get into a fistfight with her, Sally thought. Pearl did have an impressive right hook. For being so short, she would be a formidable opponent for anyone to beat. Sally headed back to her beach chair and got an idea. "We should paint coconuts."

Pearl turned back from the water. "Is that some kind of euphemism?"

"What? No." Sally shook her head and dug into her beach bag for the morning letter and unfolded it dramatically, "At 10:00 a.m., they have an art activity at the pavilion."

"Coconut painting?"

"Oh, come on. I did all your crazy stuff yesterday."

Pearl threw the rest of her roll into the water and started back to the beach. "Fine. But I'm gonna paint somethin' vulgar on mine, like a penis."

Sally's mouth dropped open. She didn't think Pearl could shock her anymore, but clearly she was wrong. "You can't do that."

"Ain't like it'll be a big penis." She pulled Sally up and looped her arm through her friend's. "Come on. We're gonna miss all the good coconuts."

17

Coconut Painting

Pearl picked up two of the coconuts from the table, held them up to her chest, and shimmied back and forth. The young man registering guests for the daily craft activity stifled a laugh. Sally rolled her eyes and batted at the coconuts, sending one of them plummeting to the ground and rolling across the sidewalk.

Pearl protested, "Hey, you just ruined my boob."

"Your boobs aren't nearly that big," Sally shot back, bending over to retrieve the runaway coconut. She held it up to the young man and said, "I guess I'll use this one." She turned it over in her hands to ensure it wasn't cracked and considered what she would do with it. She loved being creative but hadn't picked up a brush in a long time, except to paint her living room.

Pearl tucked the other coconut under her arm and motioned to Sally. "Let's find a spot."

The tables were arranged in a large rectangle, and they picked a corner on the far side of the registration table. It wasn't long until most of the seats were full except for one next to Sally.

Just as they were getting ready to start, Shannon came running up, thankfully clothed, waving her arms. "Wait for me." She grabbed a coconut from the table and made a beeline for the empty chair next to Sally.

"Great," Pearl said. "Ten bucks says she asks for a knife to turn that thing into a bikini top."

"Oh, stop," Sally said, pouring blobs of paint onto the paper plate they had each been given.

Shannon leaned over and said, "Good morning. Are you guys hungover, or is it just me?"

"Hair of the dog. Start the mornin' with a drink, and that ain't a problem," Pearl said.

Shannon laughed and smacked the table. "Ain't that the truth." She picked up each paint bottle to examine the color before selecting her palette. "What're you guys going to paint on your coconuts?"

Sally looked at her coconut again; it was a rough surface, so something super detailed wouldn't make any sense. She'd loved to paint as a kid. When they were first married, Harold had bought her an easel and a little paint set for Christmas.

She had set it up in the corner of their first apartment's spare bedroom. She'd checked out books from the library and studied different painting techniques. She had spent hours working on her first painting, a bouquet of sunflowers. After refusing to let Harold see the artwork for weeks, she'd finally dropped her paintbrush in the turpentine and stepped back. It had been ready. It hadn't been a masterpiece, but it had been a respectable first effort, and she had been proud of it, the sun streaming through the window right onto the painting.

She'd wiped her hands on her rag and smoothed the hand-kerchief covering her hair. A smear of yellow paint had cut across her cheek like war paint.

"Honey, I'm done," she'd said to Harold, who had been sitting in his plaid recliner watching the news.

Harold hadn't heard her. She'd stepped closer and said more loudly, "Honey, I'm done if you want to see it."

"Oh," he'd said, "with that painting?"

Sally had nodded and pulled on the hem of her shirt. Her hands had started to sweat. Harold had grunted as he'd gotten out of his chair, "Well, alright then. Let's go take a look."

Sally had held her breath and waited for his response. He'd tipped his head to the side and then straightened it again. Then he'd turned to her and said, "This took you all this time?"

She'd stepped closer to the easel. "Don't you like it?"

Harold had gestured. "It looks like a little kid did it."

Sally's heart had sunk. She'd blinked back tears trying to comprehend how he could have been so cruel. He had noticed her tears and groaned, "Come on, honey. I just don't want you to waste your time on something you'll never be good at." Without another word, he'd walked out of the room, leaving her standing there. Why would he have given her painting supplies just to criticize her for using them?

That had been the last time she'd painted, creatively and for herself, until now.

"I don't know," Sally said. "What about you?"

Shannon lifted the coconut to eye level and examined it. "I'm going to make it a hula girl. Just her torso, of course."

"Are you gonna put clothes on her?" Pearl asked, grinning.

"I don't know yet," Shannon said. "But I think she'll look great on the front desk back home. She can be our new resort mascot."

"If you have a resort, why are you guys down here? Don't

you have guests to take care of?" Sally asked.

Shannon's shoulders slumped. "Actually, the resort isn't all that profitable except for a couple of months in the summer. Nobody wants to be naked in Minnesota in the wintertime. We hooked up with the Flamingo Singles a few years ago and found it was a great way to supplement our income."

Sally looked over. "What do you mean by supplementing your income? I thought Flamingo Singles was a travel group?"

Shannon cleared her throat, "Oh yeah, it is, but sometimes we get asked to do things to help people back home. Chuck recruited us. You'd have to ask Dottie more about it. I don't know much about the details, I just follow along with Ricky." She shook her finger at them. "But I know we make some good money."

18

Flamingo Singles Time

Later that day, Sally and Pearl were leaving their room when Dottie's shrill laugh rounded the corner. She wore white linen shorts and an off-the-shoulder pink top with bell sleeves. Her hair twisted up at the back of her neck, and long gold earrings matched the bangles jingling on her arms. Mike walked with her, his hands shoved in the pockets of his gray linen shorts. A white button-down with the sleeves rolled up offset his tan skin.

Dottie didn't notice them as she banged loudly on the door down the hall. "Chuck, open up. You can't hide in there all day."

Mike met their eyes and shrugged. Sally smiled, and Pearl looked back and forth between them.

Dottie turned to say something to Mike and noticed he was looking at Sally and Pearl. "Oh, my," she said, pulling her hand over her heart. "What are you doing here? You spying on us or something?" She giggled.

Pearl took a step forward. "Are you doin' somethin' we should spy on?"

"Aren't you the funniest woman alive?" Dottie fanned her face with her hand and then turned back to banging on the door.

"He ain't in there," Pearl called out.

"Where is he? He was supposed to meet me an hour ago," Dottie whined. She examined her hand and rubbed her knuckle.

"No idea, but you are gonna knock a hole clean through the door. If he was in there, he would've answered by now."

Dottie clenched her fists, and her face flushed with frustration. Then she seemed to remember Mike was watching her. She rolled her shoulders back and pasted a smile on her face. "Mike, are you going to invite these ladies to join us on our little adventure?" She turned her attention to Sally and Pearl. "We are going to take the ferry to Cozumel. It's all arranged. If you come, it'll be my treat. Maybe we can even talk you into officially joining the Flamingo Singles."

Mike smiled. "If you don't have any plans the day after tomorrow, you should join us. It might be fun." He ran a hand through his hair.

"What do you think, Sally? Want to spend the day in Cozumel with Mike?" Pearl asked, smiling innocently at Sally.

Sally's face flushed. She bit her lip. Of course she wanted to go, but Mike made her feel like a schoolgirl. "What's everyone doing tonight?" Sally asked, trying to change the subject.

"We're having a picnic on the beach for dinner. It's a Flamingo Singles tradition." Dottie clapped her hands. "Actually, that would be the perfect way to initiate you two into our group."

"Now hang on," Pearl started.

Dottie ignored her and turned to pound on the door once again. After three quick raps, she gave up, sighed, and turned around. "Well, this is annoying. If you see Chuck, please tell him I'm looking for him." Sally nodded, and Dottie headed off towards the clubhouse. "Come on, Mike, we'll be late for drinks."

Mike shrugged and followed her. He shoved his hands in his pockets but then stopped and turned back. "You really should join us tonight. Eight o'clock on the beach." He tipped his head and followed behind Dottie.

Sally watched them for a minute and then turned back to Pearl. "Dinner on the beach sounds nice."

"*Hmph*. Dinner at eight? What are we, English royalty? It's ridiculous."

"But we're going, right?"

Pearl started walking. "Of course. But only so you can make googly eyes at Mike."

Sally scoffed, "I do not want to make googly eyes at anyone."

"Oh yes, you do. I need to get a snack if we ain't eatin' until bedtime. Let's find some ice cream."

They hadn't gotten very far when they heard a door open behind them. Turning around, Chuck peeked out of his doorway. His swollen, bloodshot eyes struggled to focus. The few greasy hairs he usually combed smoothly over his head were sticking up in all directions, making him look like a rabid rooster.

"What in tarnation? Didn't you hear Dottie makin' all that racket out here?" Pearl asked.

"Oh. Yeah. Well, I was... asleep." A loud belch erupted from him. "Excuse me."

"Are you okay?" Sally asked. He seemed drunk but worse. Maybe he had taken a sleeping pill with his whiskey.

Chuck leaned against the door frame to his room. "My ex-old lady is giving me hell. Even threatened to kill me. Have a bunch of screenshots. Just in case anything happens to me, she should be your first suspect."

"Really? That's awful," Sally said, her eyes wide. She couldn't imagine threatening someone like that.

"Not the first time. Listen, don't tell Dottie you saw me. She is driving me nuts. ."

"We ain't gonna lie to your girlfriend for you," Pearl said, pursing her lips.

Chuck smacked his belly and laughed. "Girlfriend? No, she is many things, but not that."

Sally was confused. "What do you mean?"

Pearl spoke up, "Never mind. We ain't wantin' details."

But Sally did want details. Something weird was going on.

Chuck leaned forward and tried to wrap an arm around Sally and bring her in for a hug. "You could be my girlfriend, though."

Sally crossed her arms and folded in on herself at the invasion of her personal space. Pearl grabbed his hand and bent it backward. "Keep your hand to yourself, or you may find it broken and that watch of yours missin'."

Chuck put his hands up defensively. "Relax. I was messing around. And this watch never leaves my wrist, not even during lovemaking."

"Stick to messin' with Dottie. Sally ain't on the market." Pearl grabbed Sally's hand and dragged her away.

That evening they headed down to the beach to meet with the group. Flames from a fire pit licked the sky and served as a beacon for the gathering. Tables and chairs surrounded the fire. Dottie noticed them and waved them over, patting the seat next to her. "Ladies, come join Mike and me. Best seats in the house." She laughed and smacked her thigh.

Sally wasn't sure if she should sit beside Mike or Dottie. She swallowed hard and walked over to the table, the sand making it hard to be graceful. Pearl chose the seat next to Dottie. Sally swallowed her nerves, smoothed her skirt under her legs, and slid into the seat next to Mike.

"So, are you enjoying your trip so far?" Dottie asked, pouring herself a glass of wine.

"Oh yes, I have always wanted to travel," Sally said.

"You're from Michigan, right?"

Sally held up her right hand to illustrate Michigan and pointed to the middle. "A small town in Michigan that's right about here."

A group of waiters appeared, carrying trays across the sand and setting covered plates in front of them. When everyone was served, they removed the covers to reveal a delectable meal of surf and turf. The conversation was replaced for the next few minutes with the sounds of dinner. It wasn't until she placed her napkin over her empty plate that Pearl asked, "What about you, Dottie? Where are you from?"

Dottie shifted in her seat and took a swig of her wine. "Born and raised in Alabama. Roll Tide." She lifted her glass in the air.

"Did you always travel?" Sally asked.

Dottie shook her head. "Um, no. I was a lawyer's wife. You know how it goes. Big house, nice clothes, a beauty pageant title." She took another drink of wine. "Look it up if you don't believe me, I was Miss Alabama 1971."

Sally nodded, impressed. She had never met a beauty queen before. And she could easily believe Dottie had worn a crown.

Dottie wasn't finished. "My life was perfect." She pulled her phone out and swiped through photos of her children and grandchildren. Sally and Pearl bit back laughter as Dottie showed them a picture of an unfortunately cone-headed baby. Dottie continued, slurring her words. "And then my husband died in a car accident on his way to a bed and breakfast with his legal assistant."

Sally tugged on the hem of her shirt and stared at the fire. She wanted to slide under the table and disappear. Luckily Pearl had no such reservations.

"Was his assistant a man or a woman?"

Dottie's mouth dropped open, and she said indignantly, "What are you trying to say?"

"Oh, ain't judgin', just curious," Pearl said flippantly.

"For your information, it was a beautiful young woman with nothing between her ears."

Pearl lifted her glass, "Ahh, to bein' young and stupid."

Dottie nodded her head in agreement and clinked her glass.

After a few moments of silence, Pearl cleared her throat and stood, "Thank ya'll for a lovely dinner. I think we're gonna head back to the room to grab a sweater." She turned to Mike. "Will you be at the bar later?"

He nodded.

"Great, we'll be seein' you there." Pearl gave Sally a pointed look, and Sally stood, giving Mike and Dottie a quick smile and following Pearl up the beach.

"Oh, we missed the Latin Fire show," said Sally as applause echoed from the courtyard.

"That's okay. We can make our own. Maybe find you a Latin lover." Pearl wiggled her hips.

"Oh, stop it." Sally waved her off.

Pearl just laughed. "Or maybe Mike will be there."

Sally's face flushed, and she couldn't think of any intelligent reply, so she just huffed.

They walked silently until Pearl said, "You know, this would be the perfect setting for a true crime story."

"What? Why do you say that?" Sally's eyes darted around the area.

Pearl shrugged. "Late night swimmin', sharks, fire. Lots of ways to off someone."

19

The Dance

When they walked up to the outdoor bar, a few people danced to a song neither Sally or Pearl recognized. Dottie perched on a seat at the bar, her legs crossed and a sequined sandal bouncing along with the music. She plucked a maraschino cherry from the drink she was holding and popped it into her mouth. Mike was standing beside her, elbows on the bar, seeming to hang onto her every word. Annoyance pricked Sally's skin. There was no denying Dottie was pretty, even before learning that she'd been a beauty queen in her youth. Sally absently touched her hair, wishing she had worn a different shirt.

While Sally was lost in thought, Pearl crossed to the bar and wedged herself between Mike and Dottie. Pearl waved her over with another big smile and a tip of her head, so Sally reluctantly crossed the floor and sheepishly smiled at Mike.

"Hi," Sally said, shifting on her feet.

"Well, hello there," Mike smiled.

"H-How's it going?" Sally stuttered.

"Uh, it's just fine. I was just here talking to Dottie. And now I'm talking to you fine ladies." Dottie scoffed behind them and seemed irritated at the interruption.

"Well, Pearl and I were going to get a drink and sit at a table. Do you want to join us?" Sally said, and Pearl looked at her and nodded in approval. Sally pulled on the hem of her shirt and sniffed. She didn't know what made her say that. It was very unlike her to be so forward.

He said, "Sure," and used two fingers to give a little salute to Dottie before following Sally and Pearl to one of the high-top tables near the edge of the dance floor.

Pearl looked at the two people on the dance floor doing some grinding dance that turned into an arm motion she had never seen before.

"What do you think they call that dance?" Sally asked Mike.

He looked at the couple for a few moments, weighing his response. "I think it's called too much tequila and not enough sex."

Sally gasped and then giggled at the audacity of his comments. People didn't talk like that in her circle at home, but as she tilted her head and considered, he was right.

Pearl smacked the table. "You nailed it," she said, pointing at him. "I think I'm gonna buy you a drink." She roared with laughter at her own joke, given it was an all-inclusive resort.

Mike said, "I'll tell you what. I'll grab the drinks. You ladies hold down the fort. I'll be right back." He took the drink orders and strode up to the bar.

As soon as he was out of earshot, Pearl leaned over. "Well, lookie here. You're gonna end up gettin' a brand new boyfriend if you ain't careful."

"Oh, stop it!" Sally said, "My husband just died, and you're telling me to get a boyfriend? I don't want a boyfriend. Besides, he was looking at Dottie. There's no way he would pick me over

Dottie."

Pearl looked at her sideways, "I don't know. He looked at you like my old hound used to eyeball a rib bone."

Sally didn't know how to respond. She'd caught him looking at her several times. But she hadn't dated in years, so how did she know if someone liked her or not? And if he did like her, well, that would be something. Sally's heart swelled and seemed to unfreeze for the first time. *And even if he likes Dottie instead, this feeling of hope is worth the trip,* Sally thought.

Mike walked back from the bar, making a show of trying to balance three drinks in two hands. Sally and Pearl laughed as they watched him cross the floor and set the drinks in front of them. "Thank you," Pearl said. "What kind of tip are you expectin'?"

Mike looked serious for a moment and turned to Sally. "I'll take a dance from you," he said. Sally just froze. Pearl looked at her like she had grown an extra head, kicked her foot under the table, and gave her a curt nod.

Sally stammered. "O-okay. Sure, that would be nice."

Mike nodded and picked up his drink, wincing at the rap song reverberating across the floor. "Let's wait for a song we recognize."

They sat, talked, and laughed as Mike told him about his childhood in Texas. "No, it's true. I used to carry the hens around the yard. They were pretty tame. But we had this evil rooster named Elvis Peckley. My mom loved Elvis." He paused to take a swig of his drink. "One day, I was outside feeding the chickens, and suddenly the rooster came out of nowhere and went after me. He chased me all over the yard. Whenever I tried to run to the house, he blocked my path. I was screaming at the top of my lungs. Finally, my dad came out of the barn with an ax. He was spittin' mad. He just walked up to that rooster and brought that ax down hard. The head landed on the ground, but I swear that thing kept chasing me. I was wailing by then. My dad scooped me up into his arms, and when that rooster's body came close, he kicked it – sent it flying like a football."

Sally and Pearl roared, wiping tears from their eyes. After another round of drinks, the DJ played a song they recognized: it was an old Righteous Brothers song, and Sally immediately tensed.

"Come on, I want to collect my dance now," Mike said, holding out his hand.

Sally's heart pounded. She managed to smile as she stood and slid her fingers into his palm. Sally turned to see Pearl beaming at her. Pearl raised her eyebrows several times. Sally mouthed "Stop it," but then pressed her lips together to suppress her smile.

Mike was a good dancer. He held her hand in his, put his other hand on the small of her back, and kept a respectful distance between them. Sally's mouth went dry as saltine crackers, so it was good that they didn't try to talk much. Every time she looked at him, he was looking at her. Her heart fluttered, and her eyes darted around the room.

About halfway through the song, she let herself relax and focused on his hand on the warmth of her back, like a beacon. Her stomach did a little flip. She laughed at herself for being nervous as a schoolgirl.

Mike looked down at her. "What?"

She just shook her head. "Nothing. I'm just having a good time."

"Me too, Sally." He gently pulled her closer, and they swayed to the music. She relaxed into him. Maybe it was the alcohol.

As she focused on her breathing, she thought, *I have to pee. Oh no, I'm in the middle of this dance and I have to pee.* She tried not to think about it and stayed focused on dancing with this handsome man.

As the song ended, Sally let out a breath, and when Mike stepped back, she felt the night chill replace the warmth of his body pressed against hers, and she shivered. Mike leaned down, his hot breath blowing across her ear. "Thank you." Then he brushed his lips across her cheek. If swooning had been something that happened in real life, she might have ended up on the floor. The last five minutes had been more romantic than the previous five years of her marriage with Harold.

Her smile faded. She was a horrible person. It wasn't fair to think so badly of Harold. When she looked back at Mike, he was searching her eyes. "Are you okay?" he asked.

She swallowed. "I'm fine. I just haven't danced like that in a long, long time,"

"Well, hopefully, it won't be so long 'til you dance like this again."

As they returned to the table, Sally couldn't help but notice Dottie watching them. Her eyes were blazing. She was stirring her drink with her little straw with so much force she sent an ice cube flying out of the glass, bouncing across the bar. Sally bit back a laugh.

They weren't at the table for a minute before Dottie slid up and used her hip to bump Mike's thigh. "Hey, how come you haven't asked me to dance?" she whined.

He said. "Oh, well, I'm a one-and-done kinda guy. So maybe another night."

"All right, but you promised!" she said, taking the brush-off

97

in stride. She turned back to the bar and wiggled her butt as she walked.

"She's as subtle as a bull in a china shop," Pearl groaned.

Mike brushed his chin with his hand. "Ah, she's not so bad. I mean, for a beauty queen."

Pearl burst out laughing. "You got that right," she said.

Mike smiled at her and said, "Ladies, I hate to do this, but I need to excuse myself. I have a couple more people I'd like to talk to tonight. I'm trying to get a volleyball game set up for tomorrow. By the way, do the two of you want to play?"

Pearl said, "Sally will!"

Sally's head whipped around in surprise.

"What? You said you were in great shape and all, so go play volleyball!"

Sally nodded. "Alright, I'll play."

"Alright. Ten o'clock. The court by the beach."

"Okay."

Mike pushed himself back against a table. "Have a good night, ladies, and stay out of trouble!" he said teasingly with a wag of his finger. He wandered over and started talking to several people from Dottie's group.

"Sally and Mike, sittin' in a tree.... " Pearl started when he was out of earshot.

"Oh, stop it. It was just a dance." Sally felt her face heating. She bit her lip. What was she doing? Harold had just died, and she was sexing it up with someone else. No more. She needed to stick with Pearl and have fun. Mike was off-limits.

20

Open Door

Sally and Pearl leaned against each other, laughing, as they rounded the corner to their room. Sally dug into her pocket for their room key. Across the hall, Chuck's door was open, a late-night talk show blaring from the television inside.

"What in the world?" Pearl asked, pulling away from Sally and heading to the doorway.

"Oh Pearl, what are you doing?" Sally asked, still digging past her wallet, ibuprofen, and phone, looking for her key in her bag.

"That door ain't supposed to be open," Pearl said, pointing to the room.

"It's not our business," Sally said, reaching out to grab Pearl's arm and missing. She just wanted to get to bed.

"Oh my stars, relax. I'm just gonna peek inside," Pearl said as she stumbled towards the door.

Sally followed Pearl into the room. Three steps in on the Mexican tile, Pearl stopped abruptly, causing Sally to crash into her from behind.

After a grunt, Sally looked around the room. A large, framed beach print was hanging cockeyed on the wall. A lamp lay on the floor, blinking like the plug had come loose. The dresser drawers were pulled out, and clothing was strewn around the room.

"Well," Pearl said, sucking in a breath.

"What in the world?" Sally stood next to Pearl, her mouth hanging open.

The light from the lamp flashed on something gold half-hidden under the bed. Sally stepped towards the bed but was distracted when the framed print slid off the nail, crashing to the ground. Both Sally and Pearl shrieked and then laughed nervously. Pearl spotted the remote on the floor and grabbed it to turn off the television.

"Chuck?" Pearl called out tentatively.

No answer.

"He's not here," Sally said, folding her arms across her chest.

"How can you tell in all this mess?"

"Maybe he had a party?" Sally offered.

Pearl grinned. "Sally Johnson, are you insinuatin' there was a swingers party here this evenin'?"

Sally gaped. "What? No. Of course not."

"Don't see any condoms." Pearl poked around the room. She opened the bathroom door. "No swingers in here."

"Stop it, Pearl. We shouldn't be in here."

"Afraid you'll be guilty by association?" Pearl teased.

Sally's face reddened. She had no idea how any of that worked. And this was Chuck's room; she didn't want to be caught wandering inside. Her skin prickled with that strange feeling again. Something wasn't right. Maybe someone got into a fight. Or perhaps Chuck was drunk again and he'd passed out somewhere on the resort.

Pearl picked her way through the room, dodging flower print shirts and plaid boxer shorts. She slid open the door to the patio. Empty. Finally, she turned to Sally and shrugged. "He ain't here."

Sally fought the urge to roll her eyes. Of course he wasn't. But he could come back at any moment. "Let's get out of here." She backed towards the door, bumping her hip on the dresser and flinching. That was going to leave a bruise.

Pearl stood between the two queen-sized beds. "Hopefully, the fool didn't decide to go for a late-night swim or somethin'. He'll end up shark food."

Sally's eyes darted around the room. They shouldn't be in here. It was probably illegal. She stood on the threshold and watched Pearl scan the room one more time before throwing up her arms and walking out. Sally pulled the door shut behind her.

"He's lucky it was us that found his room wide open. Although I don't know who would want to dig through that mess to try and find anythin' valuable."

Sally nodded and tugged on the hem of her sweater. She hoped Pearl was right. Nagging doubts hovered on the edges of her thoughts. She pushed them aside and followed Pearl to their room, locking the deadbolt behind her.

Pearl walked out of the bathroom in her purple nightshirt. She pulled back the covers on her bed and said, "That Mike was sure interested in you."

Sally was safely tucked under the covers. Her crime novel opened on the bookmarked page. Looking over her reading glasses at Pearl, she asked, "What are you talking about?"

Pearl looked at her incredulously, "You know what I'm talkin' about. And I think you like him too."

Sally slammed her book shut, "I'm not on the market for a man, at least not outside the pages of this book." She shook the text in the air for emphasis.

Pearl slid under the covers. "You might want to reconsider that stance. I bet he's got money." Pearl leaned over and flipped the switch on the bedside lamp between them.

Sally rolled on her side, leaned over, and flipped it back on. "I can't believe you said that." She was used to Pearl being blunt, but this was just rude. She was on vacation, and the last thing she wanted to do was worry about money or anything back home.

Pearl rolled on her side towards Sally and leaned on her elbow. "Look, I'm just bein' practical. And Mike seems like a nice guy."

Sally's eyes blazed. "He's a nice guy, but that's not the point."

"Then what is the point?"

Sally sat up and scooted back against the headboard. She folded her hands in front of her and looked down at her wedding ring. She struggled to find the words. What did she even want to say? She didn't know what she wanted, but it wasn't some complicated relationship. "Can't we focus on our vacation, like we said we would? I want to keep things simple."

Pearl threw the blanket back and swung her feet over the side of the bed. "Honey, I'm sorry if I made you uncomfortable." She crossed to Sally's bed and sat on the edge, patting her hand. "Let's forget I said anythin'. No more talk of money or men. Okay?"

Sally smiled. "Okay. I'm having a good time."

Pearl stood up, "Good, me too. Let's get some sleep. We got a big day tomorrow."

"What are we doing?"

Pearl did a pirouette and flopped back on her bed. "I could tell you, but I'd have to kill you." She reached over and flipped off the light.

21

Who Died?

Saturday, October 16th

Sally was still asleep when she heard a high-pitched scream outside the room. She thought it was a seagull and rolled over for another thirty minutes of rest. When she finally rolled out of bed, it was quiet, just how she liked it. She was brushing her teeth when Pearl peeked her head into the bathroom and asked, "Ain't you hearin' all that ruckus outside?"

Sally turned off the water and heard voices in the hallway. She put her toothbrush away. "What's going on?"

"No idea. I just woke up. And I gotta use the bathroom."

Sally moved out of her way and headed to the front door, opening it a sliver to see what was happening. Chuck's door was open, and a heavyset man in a dark suit and crocodile boots stood in the doorway. A toothpick hung out of the corner of his mouth, a blank look pasted on his face. A petite woman in a crisp blue dress and white maid's apron was leaning against the wall and hugging herself. Her face was ashen as a uniformed officer questioned her. A man in a suit and wearing a resort name tag stood beside her, patting her arm for support. A police photographer was snapping pictures of the building and stairs before slipping inside the room. Several police officers and resort staff members crowded around the bottom of the stairs.

"What do you see?" Pearl asked, popping open the tab on her daily medicine case.

Sally jumped and sucked in a breath. She had been so focused on what was happening outside that she hadn't heard Pearl leave the bathroom. "Some fuss in Chuck's room. Not sure. Maybe Chuck had himself a party after all." Sally moved her eyes back to the bottom of the stairs at the end of the hall. A group of officers was gathered around a puddle of blood on the concrete. Her hand flew to her heart. "Oh no."

"That don't sound good," Pearl said, rushing over to stand beside Sally and pulling the door open more. Pearl surveyed the scene and let out a low whistle.

Sally couldn't tear her eyes away from the activity at the bottom of the stairs. They must have already taken whoever's blood that was to the hospital. She followed the trail of blood up the stairs and onto the railing. What had happened? Sally turned to say something to Pearl, but her eyes caught a flash of hot pink running down the sidewalk. It was Dottie.

Dottie gasped at the blood on the ground and put a hand over her mouth before asking, "What happened?"

One of the officers, a tall man with his hair combed back, stepped forward, "Ma'am, we need you to stay back and let us do our job."

"Did that come from Chuck? Where is he?" Dottie squealed and leaned down. The officer looped his arms under her shoulders and lifted her away from the pooled blood.

"Ma'am, we don't know much yet. Please go back to your room. We will contact you if we have any questions." He tried to take her elbow and steer her away from the stairs, but she shook him off.

"I want to know if it was Chuck. Did he fall? Is he alive?" She looked up the stairs at his open door.

"Please, go back to your room or maybe to breakfast. If there is any danger, we will tell you."

"This is awful," she wailed. "I need to know if it was my friend. I want answers now."

Every officer stopped their conversation and looked at Dottie.

She sniffed. "Chuck is the nicest man. Please, tell me if he's dead." Her voice caught on the last word.

Another officer rubbed a finger under his nose and pointed to the room, asking, "You know the man staying here?"

Dottie squared her shoulders and pushed her hair out of her face, composing herself. "Yes, he and I were very close."

The officer raised his eyebrows and looked at one of the other officers, who gave him a slight nod. Then he turned back to Dottie and pointed to the grass next to the sidewalk. "Could you step over here with me?"

Dottie's eyes grew wide. "Of course. I am happy to help any way I can."

Sally and Pearl barely breathed, trying to listen to the conversation between the officer and Dottie. Unfortunately, they only caught the occasional word that meant nothing to them without context.

After a few minutes, the officer put his hand on Dottie's shoulder and spoke softly to her. She nodded, eyes downcast. Then she turned and swiftly walked away, wiping her nose on her sleeve.

Pearl pushed the door closed. "Not the kinda excitement I was lookin' for today." She crossed over and sat on the bed, grabbing her sneakers to slip on.

Sally stood frozen by the door. Her hands absently moved to her hem, rubbing it between her fingers, blinking rapidly.

Pearl noticed her apprehension and stood to take her hands. "Honey, it's okay. We ain't even sure what happened. Let's go get some breakfast and let this all blow over."

"Oh, I don't know. Is it safe to leave the room?"

Pearl turned and put her hands on her hips. "We can take the stairs around back. If I don't get somethin' to eat and take my heart medicine, my death'll be on your hands."

Sally sucked in a breath and stood. "That isn't funny."

"I ain't jokin'," Pearl said. Sally skittered around the bed and grabbed her tote.

"You shouldn't be joking about death when poor Chuck... .well, you shouldn't be joking." She pursed her lips and followed Pearl, turning to pull the door shut behind her.

The buffet line was already winding out the door, and chatter filled the air. When Sally and Pearl joined the end of the line, it was clear the entire resort knew something about the drama unfolding in the room next to theirs.

"I heard he was stabbed to death," a woman up the line said. "He isn't dead. I heard the sirens leaving the resort this morning. They don't use sirens if the person is dead."

"No, he choked to death. It was an accident."

"They don't bring out the police and crime scene tape for an accident."

Sally's eyes widened with every overheard comment. "Do you think he could have been attacked or something?" she asked Pearl.

"I don't know. I'm just not gonna assume," Pearl hissed. "It makes an ass out of you and me."

"What if he's dead? What if he was murdered?" Sally was conflicted. What if someone had been murdered in the room next to them? What if there was an actual murderer here right now? She looked around, trying to recall everything she knew about a murderer's behavior.

"Settle down. I'm sure the resort will let us know if there's anythin' to be worried about."

The chatter in the line continued even as it started to move. Sally glanced back over her shoulder towards their room, even though there were three buildings between them and the crime scene.

"Come on," Pearl said, walking through the door into the buffet.

Sally tagged along behind her. But all she could think about was the potential murder scene. She had never been involved in a crime. She had never even had a speeding ticket. Watching it on television was one thing, but this was awful. Maybe she should go home.

Pearl looked her over and said, "Listen, I'm gonna find out what happened and tell you, okay? But for now, relax. ."

Sally sat on the edge of her chair, wringing her hands. "I knew this was a horrible idea. I should have listened to my son and never come here."

Pearl shuffled over and sat across from her, patting her hands. "Honey, this ain't what I had planned either. But you can't say it hasn't been exciting." She cocked her head to the side and raised her eyebrows up and down.

Sally pulled her hands back, grabbed a jelly container for her toast, and peeled the tab. "You are crazy. Do you know that?"

"Everybody knows that," Pearl replied with a wave of her hand.

"I keep thinking about poor Chuck. I can picture his bloated purple face."

"How can you picture that? We ain't even know how he died." Pearl grabbed a roll from the breadbasket and ripped a piece off, slathering it with butter and shoving it in her mouth.

"I know, but I can't get it out of my mind. There was so much blood on the stairs and even on the railing. Shouldn't we tell them about the open door last night?"

Pearl leaned in. "You better not be thinkin' it's a good idea to tell them we were in his room, lookin' around. They could think we had somethin' to do with his fall." She shook her head. "No way."

"But what if he was murdered and they find our fingerprints in the room? Or a hair fiber? We could become suspects."

Swallowing, Pearl said, "Oh, my stars. He might be fine. He may show up at the bar tonight flashin' his gold watch and showin' off the stitches in his head, lookin' for sympathy." She looked at Sally's horrified expression and softened her approach. "Let's wait and see. And if he was killed, well, that's another story. Heck, maybe we can catch the killer and be the heroes of the resort."

"Oh, I don't know." Sally covered her face with her hands.

Pearl joined her. "Listen, let's eat our breakfast, enjoy the rest of the day, and see what comes of it. If there's some murderer on the loose, we can either hightail it outta here or help catch the creep." She tipped her head to meet Sally's eyes. "I wouldn't let anythin' happen to you."

Sally attempted a weak smile and nodded.

Pearl smiled back and then looked up, thinking. "I knew I

should've brought my gun."

Sally's mouth dropped open. "What do you need a gun for?"

"I always carry a gun at home. I feel kinda naked without it." She pointed at Sally. "You should get a gun too. I'll teach you how to shoot."

Sally shook her head. "No, thank you. I don't like guns."

"Guns don't care if you like them, but they can come in handy if you're in a bind."

22

Paper Panties

Pearl looped her arm through Sally's as they walked through the subdued resort. It was a depressing change from the upbeat party of the past few days. Approaching their building, it was clear the investigation was ongoing. "Let's go up the back again to stay outta their way. We can grab our things and head to our appointment," Pearl said, turning away from the entrance.

"What kind of appointment?"

Pearl smiled. "I'm treatin' us to a spa day."

"Oh, I don't know. It doesn't seem right to have fun when poor Chuck is laying in a hospital bed or worse."

Pearl stopped and took her arm. "First of all, he wasn't right next to us. He was in a whole other room. Second, we don't even know what happened." She caught and held Sally's gaze. "Not to be rude, but why're you takin' this so hard? We barely knew him."

Sally frowned.

"What? I said I wasn't tryin' to be rude."

Sally stared at the small cracks in the sidewalk. She wasn't sure why she was so upset about Chuck. Sally opened her mouth, unsure what she was about to say, "He, I... maybe it's just too soon after Harold." Her voice caught, and she met Pearl's eyes.

Pearl tipped her head to the side. "Gimme a hug. We didn't come here to be sad. Chuck would want us to have fun." She pulled Sally into an embrace.

Sally blinked back tears, considering. Pearl could sell sand to the ocean.

"Come on, we don't want to be late," Pearl said, grabbing her arm and pulling her along.

As much as Sally was upset by the morning's events, she couldn't help but be intrigued. She had never been to a spa. The closest she had come to it was getting pedicures and manicures before Lauren's wedding. "Really? You think it would be okay?"

"Yup. It's all arranged. The best thing we can do for Chuck is to stay out of the cops' way. Heck, we can even say a prayer for the old boy if you want to."

Sally was torn. She felt terrible for Chuck. But she didn't want to spend the rest of the trip feeling sorry for someone she barely knew. "Alright."

The spa was at the opposite edge of the resort from the next-door nudists. It consisted of three connected round wood buildings with thatched roofs. A fine mist was blowing across the entrance; it smelled like eucalyptus and something Sally couldn't quite place. Pearl pulled the door open, and a lovely young woman, her dark skin offset by a crisp white uniform, greeted them. "Welcome," she said in a smooth voice. Ambient sounds played in the background over a layer of white noise. The entire effect was one of peace and relaxation.

"Hi, we're here for the full treatment." Pearl moved her hand between Sally and herself. "She's never been to a spa before."

The young woman's smile widened, "Oh, we are so glad you are here. You are going to love it." She motioned for them to sit in two cloth-covered chairs. She handed them clipboards with waivers to fill out. Sally got to work immediately, only to be interrupted when the woman gave her a glass of cucumber-infused water. Everything was so fancy. The young woman collected the clipboards, glanced over the paperwork, and smiled. "Let's get started."

Sally swallowed and stood. She nervously pulled down the hem of her shirt. Would she have to get naked in front of this woman? Would they be in the same room? She had no idea how any of this worked. The woman motioned for them to follow, and she let Pearl take the lead as they moved through the spa back to a locker room.

"You can change here. I will be back in a few minutes to get you." She handed them each a robe and told them to put on the spa-provided disposable underwear and wait for her.

Pearl ripped open the plastic package and pulled out the pair of black oversized paper underwear. She held them up in front of her. "These are attractive."

Sally gaped. "Do we have to wear those?"

Pearl bent over and stepped into them. "You could go in your birthday suit."

Sally quickly scooped up the package and ripped it open. She stepped into the scratchy garment and tugged it up under her robe. It was like wearing a diaper. They followed the young woman down the hallway and tried to ignore the sound of their paper panties.

The young woman opened the door to a dimly lit room with the same aromatherapy mist gently blowing from a diffuser in the corner. Two massage beds sat side by side.

A pair of technicians introduced themselves as Maria and Gloria. They instructed the women to disrobe and lay face down on the tables. Then they disappeared from the room.

Sally slipped the robe off and wrapped her arms around herself, covering her chest. She slipped under the sheet, the paper panties scratching against the fabric. She kept her face turned away from Pearl to give her some privacy.

"How're you doin'?" Pearl asked, her voice muffled from talking through the table pillow.

"Okay. What happens next?" Sally wasn't sure what to expect. Would she have to be naked in front of these people? Would they oil her up like a stuck pig? She chuckled.

"What's so funny?"

Sally shook her head and then remembered Pearl couldn't see her. "Nothing."

"Just relax and let them do their thing."

Sally adjusted her hips to get more comfortable.

Three quick knocks echoed against the door, and then it opened.

"Hello, are you ready?"

"Ready as a rooster at sunrise," Pearl said.

The next hour was the most relaxing hour Sally had ever experienced. She hadn't realized how much tension she was carrying in her back and shoulders. Her body grew heavy as her muscles let go and relaxed. When she finally stood up, her legs were Jell-O. Her skin was shiny with the oils and lotions they had used, and she smelled like a mint julep.

She couldn't stop smiling as she slipped her top over her head.

This was what she'd thought vacation would be like. This was exactly what she needed. No thinking about money, or Harold, or home. Or Chuck. *Shoot.* She had already forgotten about poor dead Chuck.

"Oh my stars, that was somethin'. Those girls know their stuff."

Sally pushed the thoughts of Chuck away and tugged her shirt down. "I feel like a new woman."

Pearl smacked her arm playfully. "You look like a new woman, like a newborn baby, even. Your hair is stickin' up all over the place."

Horrified, Sally turned to the mirror and raked her fingers through her hair to tame her curls into a reasonable shape. Pearl giggled behind her. Sally whipped around and said, "Your hair doesn't look much better, you know."

Pearl bent down to tie her sneakers. "Oh, I know, but the difference is I don't care."

Sally looked in the mirror and tucked a strand behind her head. At least it wasn't sticking up anymore. She slipped her feet into her sandals and wiggled the strap between her toes.

They walked to the front desk to pay and overheard the girls talking to other guests. "I heard he died on the way to the hospital," said a man with a high-pitched nasal voice.

"That is terrible," a woman replied.

"They think he was pushed down the stairs," a petite redhead said before she noticed Sally and Pearl and stopped talking.

Pearl waited for the bill and casually asked, "They say anythin' else about Chuck?"

Sally held her breath as the others gathered around the desk and looked at each other to see who would speak first. After an uncomfortable silence, the man cleared his throat. "I don't know for sure, but I heard he fell down the stairs and hit his head. He was alive when they found him but died on the way to the hospital. Pretty bad."

Sally's mind flashed back to her living room, where the paramedics had frantically tried to revive Harold. A sheen of sweat broke out across her forehead, and her stomach roiled. Harold was dead. Chuck was dead. It was hard to comprehend.

Pearl signed the bill, and they headed back to the room. They were quiet on the way back through the resort, each lost in thought. Pearl stopped at the bottom of the stairs leading to their room and grabbed Sally's hand. She lifted her chin towards the top of the stairs, where two men in tan suits and crocodile boots were standing outside their room. One of the men was knocking loudly on the door.

"Excuse me," Pearl said as she ascended the stairs. "That's our room."

The men turned around. The taller man, with pale skin and acne pock scars, ran a finger along one side of his handlebar mustache while chewing on a toothpick. He narrowed his eyes at them. The other man, portly, with golden brown skin and oily hair combed over fiercely to the side, broke into a broad smile and said in a thick accent, "Good afternoon. We were hoping to ask you a few questions."

Pearl stopped at the top of the stairs and motioned to the room down the hall. "This is about Chuck?"

Toothpick Guy rubbed his chin and then pointed to Chuck's door. "You know him?"

Pearl leaned in as he talked, and Sally could barely make out what he was saying due to his thick accent. "Come again?" Pearl said.

Mr. Friendly touched Toothpick Guy's arm and then spoke.

"We are looking into the death of the man who stayed here. See anyone around the room last night?"

Sally bit her lip. Was Pearl going to tell them about the open room? Surely it wasn't connected to his death. He hadn't even been there. She crossed her arms and looked at the ground. Pearl would know what to do.

"You think he was murdered or somethin'? Is that why you're askin' so many questions?" Pearl asked, looking from one man to the other.

Toothpick Guy stepped forward. Mr. Friendly put his hands up in front of him. "We don't want trouble. We're just trying to do our job."

"We ain't got nothin' to say." Pearl's tone was clipped and final. Sally followed Pearl as she unlocked their room and strode inside.

Sally didn't make eye contact with them but mumbled "sorry" under her breath as she passed. Once the door was closed, Sally crossed the room, clicked on the television, and motioned for Pearl to come close. "Why didn't you tell them about last night?" she asked in a low voice.

"Why would I? There ain't nothin' to tell, and I didn't wanna get mixed up in some investigation. Besides, I don't trust those guys." She turned and kicked her sneakers off in the corner of the room.

"What do you mean you don't trust them? They're the police." Sally had been raised with a healthy respect for law enforcement.

Pearl turned to her. "Are they? You see badges? How do we know they're cops? And even if they are, that don't mean they're good cops." She shook her head and headed to the bathroom.

Sally looked back at the closed door. Was Pearl right? They hadn't shown badges. But did police in Mexico even carry badges? She stepped towards the door and peered out the peephole. The men were gone. She leaned her forehead against the door and then turned the deadbolt.

23

Ruled an Accident

Sunday, October 17th

Good Morning!

Another beautiful day is planned here at Nueva Vida del Mar. Please join us for a paint-and-pour class under the pavilion at 2:00 p.m. Bring your imagination; we will provide everything else. Tonight DJ Juan will be mixing margaritas and then hosting our Flashback Dance Party with hits from the 1980s.

We regrettably had a medical emergency at the resort yesterday. After a thorough investigation, the unfortunate passing of a guest was determined to have been an accident. Rest assured, there is no danger to any of our guests.

Please remember that the resort is home to many birds and animals. We ask that guests do not feed the pelicans or attempt to engage them. Doing so could result in serious injury.

Sincerely,

Nueva Vida del Mar

"Well, ain't that a crock of crap," Pearl said, handing the paper that had been slipped under their door during the night to Sally. They were sitting on their patio in the white plastic chairs, watching workers rake up the seaweed and scoop it into a huge pile.

"What?" Sally held a steaming cup of coffee in one hand and the paper in the other.

Pearl waved her hand dramatically. "Someone's whinin' about the stupid pelicans. Like it was my fault I got attacked."

Sally scanned the paper. "I don't think they are talking about you. It's a general statement."

Pearl leaned back in the chair and lifted her feet onto the little white plastic table. "Oh no, it's about me. I bet you all the gold in Fort Knox."

Sally looked up from the paper. "There's not much gold in Fort Knox."

"Exactly," Pearl said with a firm nod.

Sally just shook her head and went back to reading. "What do you think about Chuck?"

"The accidental death part?" Pearl asked, standing and leaning over the railing of their balcony. A gray squirrel was perched on a tree, nibbling on something they couldn't see. Pearl was stretching her fingers to try and pet the squirrel. "If you believe that, I have some oceanfront property in Arizona to sell you."

"They say it was an accident, and there's no danger to anyone."

The squirrel skittered away, and Pearl straightened. She seemed to be weighing her words carefully. Finally, she shrugged. "If they say it was an accident, it probably was."

"Why are you changing your story? You don't believe that for a minute. You've been talking about your murder theory nonstop."

"True. But I could be wrong. Unless you're thinkin' we should dig a little deeper."

"How would we do that?" Sally stood and finished the last of her coffee, making a mental note to find out what kind they served and pick some up. It was the perfect blend of beans. She savored the taste and pulled the sliding door open, the cold air blasting out of the room.

"An investigation."

Sally turned to look back onto the balcony. "A what?"

"You know, suspects, questionin', evidence." Pearl moved her hand in a circular motion. "If we find anythin', we can take it to the police. Case solved, and we'll be heroes."

"You're serious? You just agreed it was an accident."

"No, you believed it was an accident, and I didn't want you stressin' out. But his room got ransacked. There ain't no way he died fallin' down the stairs. There's blood on the railin' and the stairs. How did that get there? He was probably hit by something and then got pushed. You know, this could be fun. Our own murder mystery."

Sally bit her lip. She had always wanted to solve a crime. It could be like a game. And it wasn't like they would actually find anything. She shook her head. No, this was just the kind of trouble Joel thought she would find. "That is a ridiculous idea."

Pearl scrambled back into the room and opened drawers, looking for something to write on. "I'm gonna get started."

Sally fought off frustration. She knew Pearl would jump

down this rabbit hole and try to drag Sally with her. Not this time. "You start your investigation. I'm going to hit the gift shop."

24

So was Ted Bundy

The birds chirped in the mango grove as Sally returned to their room. Although her heart was heavy, it was hard to stay sad. It was beautiful here. She had stopped by the front office to drop some postcards for her kids in the mail. The gift shop had the perfect t-shirts for her grandkids. She knew her way around the resort by memory now and smiled at how easily this place had started to feel like home. She crossed through a break in the treeline and turned her face to the sun. A golf cart approached, and she stepped into the grass next to the path to let it pass. A young couple held hands in the back seat. They smiled and waved as they passed. Luggage was stacked on the rear of the cart and rocked when they rounded a corner. Sally smiled and waved, as if to say *welcome, you're going to love it here*.

Sally hummed to herself as she unlocked the room door, only needing to wave her card over the electronic pad once before the light turned green. Opening the door to their room, she was surprised to see Pearl standing in her bra and elastic waist shorts. Her hair was sticking up on end. She looked like a madwoman standing before the large mirror over the dresser. The pile of clothing she had been sorting had been abandoned. She held a tube of pink lipstick in her hand, but she wasn't using it for her lips.

"What are you doing?" Sally asked.

Pearl looked at her, eyes blazing. "What's it look like I'm doing?" She gestured to the mirror. It was a mess of scrawled pink letters, some words crossed out and lines drawn between others.

"I have no idea."

Pearl studied the mirror and stepped forward to write something else. "This is a list of suspects." She turned to Sally, "We're gonna figure out who killed old Chuck."

Sally wasn't sure what to say. Her dearest friend had lost her mind. A wave of concern washed over her. "Are you okay?"

Pearl was still studying the mirror. "What? Why?" she said, turning to Sally.

"You're standing in front of a mirror, but have you seen yourself?"

Pearl turned to her and put her hand on her hip. "Oh my stars, we got more important things to worry about than my hair."

Sally stepped closer to the mirror and tried to understand what Pearl was doing. There was a list of names on one side and Chuck's on the other. Lines were drawn with notes on known locations during the murder, the relationship to Chuck, and any evidence Pearl deemed essential. She had seen enough cop shows to know they needed more proof.

"What did Chuck say his ex-wife's name was again?" Pearl asked, tapping her finger on her chin.

"I think it was Kathy or Karen." Sally crossed her arms in

front of her.

"Right, Kathy." Pearl leaned over the dresser on tiptoe and added *Kathy* to the list of suspects. "Chuck said she had threatened to kill him, remember?"

Sally tried again. "Pearl, didn't they rule his death an accident?"

Pearl stomped her foot. "Oh, my stars. Ain't you payin' attention at all?"

Sally recoiled. "What do you mean?"

Pearl exhaled and calmed her tone. "How did they say Chuck died?"

Sally thought back to the exact wording she had read. "They didn't, but it's pretty clear he fell down the stairs and died," She choked on the last word.

"And..."

"And he probably hit his head on the concrete or something."

"Hmm," Pearl said, shaking her head. "Was he facin' up or down when he fell?"

"I don't know. Why?" Sally said. She hated playing games, and Pearl was making her feel stupid.

"Don't you remember the Peterson case? If someone fell down the stairs, they would land with a face plant." Pearl smacked her hand on the dresser. "But if they were pushed, they would land face up. Not to mention the blood on the stairs and railing. If he hit his head at the bottom, why was he bleeding on the way down?"

"Okay, but..." Something caught her eye, and Sally's mouth dropped open, "Why is Mike's name up there?" Her brows knitted together. They had already talked about this. "Mike is nice to everyone."

"So was Ted Bundy," Pearl replied.

Sally's eyes widened, and then she squinted. "That doesn't make any sense." She shook her head and hugged herself tighter. She liked Mike. How bad was her judgment if she thought a potential murderer, or even a serial killer, was nice? No. Mike was a good guy. She was sure of it. Okay, she was pretty sure.

Pearl tipped her head back and sighed. "Sally, this is a list of suspects." She circled her arm in front of the mirror. "We gotta include everyone and rule them out one by one. You act like you never saw a murder show."

"Fine." Sally considered the list. "If, and that's a big if, he was murdered, it was probably his ex-wife."

Pearl grinned. "Right. He said she threatened to kill him. Maybe she finally snapped."

Sally nodded. "Exactly. But where is she? We don't even know if she's in Mexico."

"Not yet, we don't." Pearl tapped her head with the side of the tube of lipstick. "But we're gonna find out."

Sally's heart sank. She knew she was being childish, but she had been looking forward to today's excursion. They were supposed to take the ferry with the Flamingo Singles. "We aren't going to Cozumel?" Sally asked, although she already knew the answer.

Pearl looked at her in disbelief. "We are all that's standin' between Chuck's murderer and justice. We can't run off to Cozumel, if that trip's even still on with one of the group leaders dead as a doornail. We only got three days to solve this crime. We gotta focus on gatherin' evidence." She fixed her eyes back on the list, then relented. "Fine, maybe we can go play bingo this afternoon."

Sally relaxed. It was probably best not to leave the resort

anyway. They were safe–as long as Pearl didn't get them killed.

25

Bingo

Pearl was true to her word. The artificial palm leaf blades hummed as they worked to push air around the activities pavilion. Other than the slight breeze created by the fans, the air was still and pregnant with moisture. Sally sat in the second row of tables that had been pushed into rows for the afternoon game of bingo. She rested her bag on the chair next to her. Pearl had insisted on stopping by the front office to request more towels, and Sally had gone ahead to ensure their seats were reserved.

Sally watched the staff scramble to set up the bingo ball cage and board. She pursed her lips. They were late. There was no way this was going to start in fifteen minutes. They hadn't even started selling cards yet. She folded her arms and huffed. Bingo wasn't just a casual activity for old ladies, it was serious business.

How many hours had she spent in smoke-filled church basements hovering over her cards, hoping for one more number?

Lost in thought, Sally jumped when a bag dropped onto the

table next to her. Looking for the source of the interruption, she found Pearl standing over her with her hands on her hips. "You getting' heatstroke or somethin'?"

Sally blinked rapidly, "What?" She had been lost in thought, and melancholy had threatened to creep in.

"Been sayin' your name for about five minutes. You were zoned out." She waved a hand in front of Sally's eyes.

Sally leaned back, cleared her throat, and looked around, grounding herself in the present. She brushed the hair off her face and pulled forth a lighthearted tone when she said, "Oh, I was just thinking about how nice it's going to be to beat you at bingo." She smiled as Pearl scraped the chair against the wood floor and sat down.

"Psh... you couldn't beat me at bingo if you had a farmer, a dog, and a lucky penny in your shoe." She pulled the straw hat from her head and dropped it on the table next to her bag. "I need a drink. I'll get you one too." She pointed at Sally as she stood and headed to the bar.

The staff finished setting up the game, and a line of players was forming to buy cards. Sally hopped out of her chair so quickly that it tipped back and clattered to the floor. She grabbed the bills she had pulled out and dug around her purse for a few more to buy cards for Pearl.

A flash of pink caught Sally's eye, along with a jolt of high-pitched laughter. It was Dottie, of course. She was weaving through the tables towards the back of the line, smiling and waving at everyone she knew. She didn't look like someone who had just lost a close friend. She didn't seem to be grieving at all, but who was Sally to judge someone's grief? She was probably still in the denial phase.

"Hey girl," Dottie said to Sally when she joined the back of the line. "Cute top."

Sally looked down at her plain navy shirt, frowned, and mumbled, "Thanks."

Dottie blew out a breath and leaned over, her face falling. "It's been such a terrible few days." She shook her head. "We had to cancel the Cozumel trip today because of what happened. Everything's falling apart."

She looked pitiful as she bit back tears. Sally clasped her hand and said, "It is awful. I'm so sorry."

Dottie nodded and slipped her hand from under Sally's fingers, using it to wipe her eyes and fan her face. "Whew, enough of that. There's no crying at bingo."

Sally shifted on her feet, not sure how to respond. She patted Dottie on the arm and scanned the room for Pearl. Where was she? It was probably better that she wasn't here. Dottie was obviously in a fragile state, and Pearl might launch into an interrogation right in the line for bingo cards.

Luckily, when Pearl did reappear with drinks in tow, Sally already had their cards set up, and Dottie was perched on the other side of the room with some of the Flamingo Singles, deep in conversation. Good. Once bingo started, there would be no chance for an awkward conversation between Pearl and Dottie. Talking during bingo was tantamount to farting in church.

Just before the first number was called out, Pearl leaned over and said, "Keep an eye out for anythin' suspicious."

Sally nodded. Around them erupted a chorus of "Shhhh," and clicking tongues. Sally dipped her head, and her face flushed. Pearl twisted one side of her mouth and shook her head in disgust.

Sally spent the next hour blissfully lost in the game. She used her dabber to scan her cards each time a number was called.

Sighing each time, she made a pass with no color added to her paper sheets. She needed her good luck charms. Unfortunately, they were tucked at home in her bingo bag.

Collective groans filled the pavilion when someone across the room yelled, "Bingo!" Pearl swore under her breath and grabbed her paper card sheet, dramatically crumpling it into a ball. "Well, ain't that as worthless as gum on a boot heel?"

Sally folded her sheets and stood to deposit them in the can at the end of the table.

Pearl followed, leaning in towards her ear. "Did you get a look at Dottie? She don't look like the grievin' friend, now, does she?"

"I suppose not, but she could be putting on a brave face."

Pearl huffed and shook her head. "That dog don't hunt."

After depositing their papers in the trash, they headed over to order another drink at the bar.

Behind them, Dottie called out, "Pearl, Sally, hold up."

Sally and Pearl turned to see Dottie hurrying towards them. She skidded to a stop and moved her hand across her heart, panting. "Whew, so glad I caught you two. We are having a memorial tonight for poor Chuck. It is going to be on the beach at seven. I hope you can come. It's just so awful, and the group needs closure, you know?"

Sally and Pearl shared a look. "Of course, we wouldn't miss it," Pearl said with a nod.

Pearl elbowed Sally until she spoke, "Um, yeah, we'll be there."

Sally hadn't brought anything appropriate for a memorial service and stood in front of her closet, weighing her options, before deciding on simple navy capris and a matching jacket. Pearl had pulled on a black pair of pants and a Hawaiian print top.

At 6:45, the sun was thinking about setting when Sally sank her toes into the still-warm sand. A small group of people was seated in chairs arranged in a semicircle around a podium set in the sand.

"How nice that they were able to set all this up," Sally said.

"Now remember, we are here for one reason," Pearl said, holding up a finger.

Sally gave her a warning look.

"Okay, two reasons," Pearl said, "Honor Chuck, but also to try and figure out who killed him."

Sally's foot landed on a sharp rock in the sand, causing her to suck in her breath and put her arm on Pearl's shoulder for balance. "Ouch."

"What'd you do?" Pearl said, watching Sally inspect the bottom of her foot.

"It's fine. Just stepped on a rock."

"Alright then," Pearl said, shaking Sally's arm off.

There was no blood, but it still ached when Sally put her foot down. She hobbled behind Pearl to where Dottie was now standing behind the podium, shuffling papers. A small black speaker was next to the podium, playing an acoustic version of "My Way."

Shannon and Ricky sat in the front row. Ricky was dressed in a black motorcycle t-shirt and Shannon was in a plain black t-shirt and jean shorts. Their fingers were laced together and resting on Ricky's knee. When Shannon saw Sally and Pearl, she gave them a weak smile.

Sally gave Shannon a small wave and slipped into a row in the back.

"Good choice," Pearl whispered. "We can keep an eye on

everyone from here. The guilty party is bound to slip up at some point."

Promptly at seven, Dottie lifted the microphone to her mouth and cleared her throat. The group did a last-minute round of shifting in their seats and wrapping up conversations. Then they turned to Dottie and solemnly gave her their attention.

"Thank you all for coming. Tonight, we honor the life of Chuck Dickman."

Pearl stifled a laugh with the back of her hand and turned it into a cough when Shannon turned to frown at her, mascara already running down her face. Sally smacked Pearl's arm.

The next thirty minutes were full of Dottie lamenting about the loss of her dear friend. She even sang "Wind Beneath My Wings" set to a karaoke track, the crowd cringing as she struggled to hit some of the notes. Then Ricky, Shannon, and several others got up to talk about how much they adored Chuck.

Sally tried to look for signs of guilt in each of the speakers. Each of them only had heartfelt things to say about their departed companion.

"The only thing he loved more than this group was his best friend, Spike, who probably doesn't even know yet. It's just so horrible," said a redhead in an American flag shirt, dabbing her eyes.

As Shannon spoke about Chuck's dancing skills and soft hands, Ricky shifted in his seat and covered his mouth with his hand. His face flushed red, and he frowned when she walked back to her seat sobbing. Why did Ricky have such a problem with Shannon and Chuck when they were supposed to be a free-love couple? Maybe he had something to do with Chuck's death.

After the speeches, Dottie made them all stand in a circle and hold hands. Sally stifled a laugh when everyone raised one foot off the ground and began to recite what she called the Flamingo Singles Pledge, their voices solemn.

> *We are the Flamingos,*
> *Loyal, brave, and true!*
> *We are the Flamingos,*
> *Loyal, brave, and true!*
> *Pink is for the sunset,*
> *And the love we seek to find,*
> *Don't mess with a Flamingo,*
> *We'll kick your ugly behind!*

At the conclusion, everyone raised their hands and cheered. Pearl caught Sally's eye, and they both burst out laughing. When they were safely back in their room, Pearl said, "That was the dumbest pledge I ever heard."

"Was it a pledge? I am not sure that's an accurate description."

Pearl shook her head. "She must've written it when she was drunk."

"Did you see anything suspicious?" Sally asked, slipping off her jacket and hanging it in the closet.

"Nothin' obvious. You?" Pearl slipped on a headband and turned the water on.

Sally pulled her capris down and kicked them off. "Only Ricky. He was pretty upset about the speech Shannon gave. He looked mad."

"Oh yeah, I saw that," Pearl said, splashing water on her face.

"Think Shannon was in on it?"

Sally sat on the edge of the bed and considered. "No. She was so upset tonight. I don't think she noticed how angry Ricky was, either."

Grabbing her pajamas from the floor beside her bed, Pearl said, "Looked like he was gonna blow a gasket. He is definitely at the top of my suspect list."

26

An Invitation

Monday, October 18th

Looking through the peephole, Sally saw Mike standing outside the door, hands shoved into the pockets of his khaki shorts. She ducked into the bathroom and pulled her lips back to check her teeth. Clean. She tugged on the hem of her shirt and opened the door. "Mike, hi."

Mike looked up under his lashes, almost seeming shy. He smiled and said, "Hey Sally. I wondered what you were up to today."

"Oh, we are just relaxing. What about you?" She looked back over her shoulder to Pearl.

Mike looked past her and then nodded. "I was heading over to the restaurant. Do you have breakfast plans yet?"

Sally shifted on her feet. Was he asking her out? Was he trying to get them to have breakfast with the singles group? "Um, I don't think so."

"Good. Would you and Pearl like to join me? I was going to grab a bite."

Sally's heart fluttered. "Oh, I don't know. Let me ask Pearl. Um," she looked back into the room. Should she invite him in? Make him wait outside?

Luckily he rescued her from that decision. "No problem. I have to grab something from my room. I'll stop back by here in a few minutes."

Sally's shoulders relaxed. She nodded and smiled.

"Who was that?" Pearl asked, watching Sally close the door.

"It was Mike. He wants us to go to breakfast with him."

"Us?" Pearl's mouth twisted mischievously.

"Oh, for heaven's sake, yes, us. He is going to stop back for an answer."

Pearl dramatically flopped on her bed and threw her hand over her eyes. "I'm feelin' a little peaky. Better go on without me."

Sally wasn't sure if she should be worried or annoyed. She put her hands on her hips. "Is this a trick to get out of going?"

Pearl moaned loudly. "Oh, just need to rest for a spell. You go without me."

"Wait, are you sick?"

Pearl's hand slid off her face. "I am sick of you askin' so many questions, detective. Don't look a gift horse in the mouth. I ain't goin' nowhere."

Sally weighed whether she should change her clothes or not. It wasn't a date or anything, so she shouldn't look like she tried too hard. But when was the last time she had breakfast with a man she wasn't related or married to? She couldn't remember.

Sliding open the closet, Sally considered her choices. She ran her fingers over the white button-down. Maybe she should wear her black t-shirt with rhinestones around the neckline. Then her eyes landed on the pale yellow dress. She lifted the hanger from the rod and held it in front of her. It was perfect. But would it seem like she was trying too hard?

"Yes."

"What?" Sally said over her shoulder.

"Wear it. You'll look like a summer day."

Sally turned, keeping the dress at arm's length. "Oh, I don't know."

Pearl sat up. "It ain't a prom dress. Just put it on. It's a perfectly reasonable choice."

Sally's mouth twisted as she thought. She shook her head to clear out the doubt. Without any more thought, she charged into the bathroom and undressed. What was the big deal? It was just breakfast with a lovely friend. Once the dress was on, she pulled on the waistline to straighten it out. Then standing in front of the mirror, she stared at her reflection. The dress perfectly set off her tan. It was nice, but not too nice.

After slipping on her leather sandals, she sat on the edge of her bed and waited. Pearl clicked on the television, and a Mexican telenovela filled the screen. A tall blonde in a curve-hugging red dress charged toward a mustachioed man with a big butcher knife. Her face and eyes were full of rage and her scream was parried by a string of rapid Spanish from the man. The woman thrust the blade forward and missed as he spun to the side. She lunged at him again; this time, her aim was true, and the knife sank into his chest. He stumbled backward as she stood her ground, chest heaving. He melodramatically fell onto a velvet settee and stretched an arm out to her before dying.

"He probably deserved it, " Pearl said before clicking to a famous American movie with Spanish subtitles.

"She had better hide that knife and clean up any fingerprints."

"A woman scorned is a dangerous thing." Pearl crossed her ankles and pulled the blanket over her legs.

"Do you want me to turn the air down before I go?" Sally asked.

"No, I like it cold."

Sally tapped her fingers on the bed. Her stomach growled. Where was Mike? She glanced back at the closet. Maybe she should change.

"Don't change. You look great." Pearl said.

How did she do that? It was like she was a mind reader.

Three rapid knocks beckoned her to the door. She smoothed her skirt as she walked. Through the peephole, she saw Mike, who had also changed from the gray t-shirt to a blue button-down. Sally smiled and pulled open the door.

"Hi. You two ready to go?"

Sally's face fell. "Oh, it's just going to be me."

Mike pulled his shoulders back. "Is everything alright?"

"Oh yes, Pearl's just tired."

As Sally stepped out of the room, she couldn't help but stare at the red police tape covering the door across the hall. Her mouth went dry. Chuck. He had been there two days ago, and now he was lying in a morgue somewhere. What did they do with the bodies of people who died on vacation? If she and Pearl did find something, would the police even believe them?

27

Thanks for Asking

Mike cleared his throat. "Are you having a nice time?"

Sally looked up from her menu, thankful for the diversion. "Yes, it's been a great vacation. Well, until yesterday."

Mike knitted his brows together in confusion, waiting for her to continue.

"I mean, with the unfortunate death of Chuck. Your group must be so upset."

Mike lifted his cup of coffee to his lips, considering how to answer. When he placed the cup back on the table, he ran his finger around the rim. "Yes, everyone was understandably upset. But when you are in a group of senior singles, it comes with the territory."

"What does?"

"People passing away. He ate like a teenager and drank like a college student. I thought he might have a heart attack or a stroke sooner rather than later."

Sally shook her head. "How awful."

Mike nodded in agreement and then frowned. "Instead, he fell down the stairs and died of a closed head injury and multiple fractures, at least according to the rumors."

Sally hadn't known about the broken bones. How had Mike found that out? Maybe Dottie had told him. As the name passed through her thoughts, Sally frowned.

Mike reached across the table and took her hand. "Let's not talk about this. I am glad we have a chance to spend some time alone together."

Sally's breath caught in her throat. She had never had someone look at her like he was. She looked down at their hands. Her gaze had to follow her hand up her arm to her shoulder to remind her that this was real. He was here with her and holding her hand. How wonderfully strange. She looked back and met his eyes briefly and then glanced away. "I bet you say that to all the girls."

Before he could respond, the waiter approached and asked for their order.

They continued their small talk, but Sally tried to think of something to say as the conversation trailed off.

"Pearl thinks someone murdered Chuck." What was she thinking? What had made her say that out loud?

"What?" Mike asked, setting his fork down.

Sally tried to backpedal. "Oh, I am sure she was joking. I mean, who would murder Chuck?"

"What do you think?"

Sally paused. "Oh, I don't know."

"Does Pearl have any theories?"

"She's a bit of a true crime junkie. You know how they are. She has multiple theories," Sally said. She straightened her silverware and looked at the table.

Mike sipped his coffee. "I hope she just stays out of it."

"What do you mean?" Sally met his gaze.

It was Mike's turn to backpedal. "Nothing. It's your first big vacation, and I wouldn't want you to waste it chasing ghosts."

Sally leaned back. Who was he to tell Pearl to back off? She was getting tired of being told what to do and think. "Pearl cares about people. And besides, we both love true crime. If we can make sure Chuck gets justice, it will be worth it."

Mike folded his arms on the table and leaned forward. "Right, but it was an accident."

"Are you sure?" It sounded more defensive than she meant, but how did he know?

"Am I sure? I wasn't there, but I trust law enforcement to do their job." His response had a bite to it.

Sally fidgeted in her chair. "Fine, maybe you are right. Let's talk about something else."

"Okay, tell me about yourself."

Sally cupped her water glass. "There's not much to tell. I was married. I have three children. My husband died earlier this year, and here I am."

"I am sorry about your husband. How long have you and Pearl been friends?"

Sally smiled. "It feels like forever, but I met her about ten years ago at bingo. We've been friends ever since."

"She seems like quite a pistol."

"She is. She is the perfect best friend, though. I wouldn't be here if it wasn't for her."

"You two could get into some trouble, I think."

Sally lifted her glass of juice to her lips and shook her head. "Not me. My life is quite boring."

"It doesn't sound boring. And even if it is, there's something to be said for boring."

Sally considered. She had lived a comfortable life for the

most part. If she didn't have some excitement now, she never would.

Sally was relieved to see the waitress approach their table with food. She didn't want the conversation turning back to Chuck.

The rest of the meal passed with light conversation. Neither of them brought up Chuck again. She wanted to ask him about his life but knew it would lead to more questions, and talking about her life made her hands sweat. She had no idea what her future would look like and didn't want anyone to feel sorry for her.

Mike set his napkin on the table as they finished breakfast and held her gaze. "Thanks for joining me."

Sally smiled shyly. "Thanks for asking."

"Do me a favor," he said, leaning in. "Get Pearl to let this situation with Chuck go. She seems like someone who has difficulty minding her own business, and I don't want trouble to find her, or you." He leaned back and pushed his chair away from the table. "Shall we go?"

Sally smiled weakly, but inside, she seethed. Who did he think he was? He didn't know them. Why was he trying so hard to get them to stop asking questions? Maybe he was the killer. Charming, good-looking, didn't that describe most killers?

He followed her out of the restaurant. When he leaned over her shoulder to push open the door, he whispered, "Don't get me wrong, I like Pearl. But Chuck's death isn't a tree worth barking up."

Sally narrowed her eyes, gave him a quick goodbye, and left him standing in the restaurant's doorway.

28

I'm Fine

Sally rolled her shoulders and tried to shake off the negativity of the breakfast. She hated leaving things so awkward. Maybe she would stop by Mike's room later and apologize. She could do that. It would be fine.

Rounding the corner, she ran into Juan. He was leaning against the yellow stucco wall of the gift shop, soaking in the sun and staring at his phone. He glanced up, caught Sally's eye, and smiled. "Ahh... the voice of an angel."

Sally smiled at the unexpected compliment. "Thank you."

"I know you can sing, but can you dance?" He shoved his phone into his pocket, slid into a salsa step, and reached out a hand to Sally. Sally laughed and let herself be pulled tight against his frame while he swiveled his hips. Her face flushed red as she realized their bodies were touching in all the places. He didn't seem embarrassed at all. Soon he spun her out to the end of his arm.

When he released her, she pulled at the waist of her dress and ran her hands along the front to smooth it out. An unexpected wave of melancholy hit her square in the chest. She forced a smile and bowed, then turned away from Juan so he wouldn't see her tears. She would hate for him to think it had anything to do with him. She gave him a quick wave over her shoulder but didn't turn around.

What was wrong with her? She hadn't broken down like this since the early days after Harold's death. Now her hands felt numb, and her heart pounded in her ears. Around the corner between two buildings, she stopped and put her hands on her knees, trying to catch her breath. She choked back a sob. Harold. Her Harold. She'd loved him despite all his flaws. And he had loved her despite all of her flaws. Maybe she could have been a better wife. How much time had she spent resenting him instead of trying to understand him? It didn't excuse his behavior, but she still loved him.

Out of the corner of her eye, she saw Dottie in her pink bathing suit hustling over, her face full of concern as she approached. "Sugar, are you okay?"

Sally forced herself to stand tall and take a deep breath. "I'm fine. Just a little winded."

Dottie persisted. "Are you sure? You look pale."

Sally forced out a chuckle. "I am sure. I need to catch my breath."

Dottie frowned. "Well, we don't need to lose anybody else, so if you start feeling sick again, go to the medical center, promise?"

Sally nodded.

Dottie put a hand on her shoulder. "Good." Then she sauntered off towards the bathrooms. The sway of her hips earned her attention from men along the way. She must have been downright dangerous when she was younger. What was it like to be the girl that turned heads in every room she walked into? And she was nice, so Sally couldn't even dislike her for it.

Sally pulled herself up straight and headed back to her room. Pulling out her card key, she could hear the television blaring through the door. When she entered, Pearl immediately muted the sound, eager to hear all about the breakfast date. When Sally recounted her conversation with Mike, Pearl was furious. "Who does he think he is? Tellin' us what to do." Pearl stomped around the room, indignantly scooping up her clothing that littered the floor.

Sally sat on the bed, drawing circles with her finger. "I think he's just worried we'll get in trouble or something."

Pearl stopped. "How? It ain't like we murdered anybody."

"We don't know that anyone was murdered. Mike confirmed he died of a closed head injury after accidentally falling down the stairs."

"And you believed him?"

"Don't be rude."

"I ain't bein' rude." Pearl stood in the middle of the room with her arms full of clothing. "*He's* bein' rude, which is surprisin'. I thought he was a nice southern boy."

"He is nice. He is just concerned. He told us to stay out of it because he doesn't want anything bad to happen."

"Maybe he killed Chuck." Pearl licked her lips and frowned. Sally shook her head. "Oh, stop it."

"What? You don't know him." she dropped the clothing on the bed. "Besides, his concern could be a red herrin'. "

Sally picked at a piece of thread on the comforter. "Are you sure this investigation is a good idea?"

Pearl glared at her. "Stop bein' such a chicken. You like this stuff as much as I do."

"Watching shows on television is not the same as getting

mixed up in something that is none of our business."

Pearl continued to sort through her clothes. She picked up a shirt, sniffed it, and wrinkled her nose before tossing it on the floor.

Sally needed some air. She also wanted to go find Mike so she could apologize. "I'm going for a walk. I want to pick up more sunblock from the gift shop."

"You could probably get a better deal at the market in town."

"Probably, but I don't want to go to the market in town. I promised Lauren I wouldn't leave the resort."

Pearl looked up. "I'm starvin'. I'll go with you, and maybe we can stop and grab me a burger after?"

Sally smiled and relaxed on her bed as Pearl flitted around the room, throwing on clothing and running a brush through her hair. Ten minutes later, they were out the door. At the bottom of the stairs, Sally remembered her plan to apologize to Mike and asked Pearl if they could stop by his room on the way.

"You don't owe him nothin'."

"If you want food, we are stopping by his room."

Pearl snorted. "Fine."

Mike's door was open, and a housekeeping cart was parked outside. Sally stopped short when she realized his room was being cleaned, so he wasn't there. She turned to leave when out of the corner of her eye, she saw the same housekeeper that had found Chuck dropping an arm full of towels into the basket on her cart.

Sally froze. "That's the woman who found Chuck."

"We gotta know if she found him face-up or face-down. Let's go ask her."

"We can't do that."

"You got a better idea?"

Before Sally could open her mouth, Pearl was already three strides ahead of her.

"Excuse me," Pearl said as the housekeeper pulled Mike's door closed. Sally sighed and followed, standing silently behind Pearl.

The housekeeper jumped, and her hand flew to her chest. She turned around.

"I'm so sorry. I didn't mean to scare you. Do you speak English?"

The housekeeper nodded. "Do you need towels?" she asked in a thick accent.

Pearl shook her head, "No, I was hopin' to ask you a question."

"Okay."

"We saw you the other mornin' when they found Chuck at the bottom of the stairs."

The woman made the sign of the cross and nodded. Sally pulled at the hem of her shirt. Pearl continued, "Yes, well, I was wonderin', was Chuck lyin' on the ground face-up or face-down?"

"Oh, it was terrible. I cannot get it out of my mind. His eyes were open and staring at the sky."

Sally bit her lip. Why did they need to traumatize this poor woman?

"Was anythin' weird about him?"

"No. I think he was going out when he fell. He was dressed nicely and had on good shoes."

"Anythin' else?"

"A gold chain around his neck and... a gold ring on his hand. I remember because it had a black stone in the middle."

Pearl crossed her arms and tapped her finger on her chin. "So he was wearin' shoes and clothes, a necklace and ring, but no watch?"

The woman nodded.

"That's all you can remember?" Pearl asked.

The woman's brows knitted together, and she shook her head. "I must get back to work."

"Of course. Thank you," Pearl said, patting the woman on the shoulder. She took a step backward and turned towards Sally, beaming and tapping two fingers on her wrist where a watch would sit.

This was too much. What was happening to their fun vacation?

29

Why Pearl Persists

Sally watched Pearl finish the last bite of her burger, a plate from the buffet balanced on her legs. Pearl wiped her hands on a napkin, set the plate on the nightstand, and stood. "Let's go."

"Did you decide on an activity?" Sally grabbed her shoes. She was torn between the dancing and cooking classes. "I thought the salsa-making class looked fun."

Pearl's mouth twisted in confusion. "Salsa? We ain't got time for that. We got a murder to solve."

Sally shook her head. "Can't we have some fun? If there were anything suspicious about his death, the police would have found it."

Pearl folded her arms, "Really? Is that why they got a whole channel on cable about cold cases?" She shook her head.

"I just don't want to get into any trouble."

"What's the worst that could happen?" Pearl asked, throwing her hands in the air.

An image of herself lying face up at the bottom of the stairs, with lifeless eyes, flashed in Sally's mind and stopped her breath. Real fear gripped her heart and held her hostage until she blurted out, "No, I'm not doing this anymore. I want to go home. I miss my kids and my nice safe life."

"Your safe life? You're bein' a coward," Pearl spat.

Sally flinched at the accusation. "Just because you don't have anybody to get home to-"

Pearl's eyes narrowed, and she pulled her chin into her neck. Sally immediately shut her mouth. Pearl said through gritted teeth. "You don't know what you're talkin' about."

Sally dropped her shoes on the floor and turned to face Pearl. "Okay, then tell me. You never talk about yourself or your family. Why?"

Pearl stomped across the room, ripped a tissue out of the box, blew her nose, threw it away, and spun around. "Fine. I don't got anybody at home, but it wasn't always that way. I had two children, and you know what happened to them? They died. Okay? I don't like talkin' about it because it won't change nothin'. So why bother?"

Sally's mouth hung open in shock. "What?"

Pearl waved her off and paced. "Look, it happened a long time ago. There's nothin' to be done about it now. I don't got anybody at home, but it ain't my fault. Alright? It is what it is and we gotta focus on the present."

Sally tried to process the fact that Pearl had children who had died. It was too awful for words. She could hardly imagine losing a child, let alone both children.

Pearl stopped and faced Sally. "And you know what else- you act like you're the only one with problems, but I got problems too. I just don't feel like talkin' about 'em all the time."

Sally felt like she'd been smacked.

Pearl folded her arms and set her jaw. She had always come

across as strong and independent. Now she stood there, chest heaving and blinking back tears, on the verge of breaking down.

Sally's throat bobbed. Pearl was her best friend and had suffered unimaginable pain. What could she say to make her feel better? Nothing. Not really. Instead, she dared to ask, "What were your children's names?"

Pearl pursed her lips and said nothing for a long moment, and then she said, "Josie and Jeff." Their names seemed foreign on her tongue. "They died of carbon monoxide poisonin' while they napped, and I was in the yard readin'." Pearl's lip quivered.

Sally wasn't sure what to say, so she just sat quietly.

"And to make things worse," Pearl continued bitterly, "They thought I had somethin' to do with it. They thought I had killed my children. It took weeks for them to figure out what had happened."

"You can't be serious."

She nodded and flopped on the edge of the bed. "I am. The police questioned me, and even threatened to arrest me. The town gossips started waggin' their tongues, and I couldn't leave the house except to go to my children's funeral. And even then, I sat in the front row knowin' everybody in town thought I'd done it. Turns out it was a defective furnace. But nobody got held to account."

"I can't even imagine. I'm a horrible friend. All this time, and I had no idea."

"But how would you have known?" Pearl said, putting her hand over Sally's. "I never tell anybody because I don't want it to - see? There you go, look at your face! You're all sad and mopey, and now the rest of the night's wrecked over somethin' that happened forty years ago. We can't fix it. We gotta move on."

"I know, but it's so sad!"

Pearl stood and walked to the poster board, keeping her back to Sally. "Alright, listen: I loved my children. I had great hopes for them. And you know what?" She turned around. "It just wasn't meant to be. God had other plans. Fine. Whatever. We're still here. If you ain't busy livin', you're on your way to dyin'.'" She walked across the room to grab another tissue. "That's why I think we should do what needs to be done right now. Stay focused on the task, and don't go worryin' about all kinds of stuff that happened that we can't do anythin' about."

Sally thought for a moment. "All right, what do you want to do?" They could do this. Sally had seen just as many true crime shows as Pearl. In a way, they had been preparing for this for years.

Pearl paused in front of Sally. She took a deep breath and let it out. She pushed her hands down and away from her body as if expelling the pain of the last few minutes, pushing those memories back where she thought they belonged. "Okay, here's what we're gonna do. We gotta figure out who did this. I know with every fiber of my bein' that this wasn't an accident. I don't know who did it. But we're fixin' to find out. We're goin' to go on and question every one of those Flamingo Singles 'til we get to the bottom of this. By any means necessary." She looked at Sally and pointed her finger. "Whatever. It. Takes." she said in short, clipped words.

30

Get in Loser

Instead of salsa-making, they had found the true crime channel on the hotel television and enjoyed a few hours of programming in the air conditioning to get themselves in the mood for crime fighting.

Later that evening, they sat at the bar under the thatched roof. Sally sipped water and watched Pearl typing furiously on her phone. "What are you doing?"

"Tryin' to figure out who Chuck's ex-wife Kathy is so we can track her down," Pearl replied without looking up.

"Why would she want him dead?" Sally asked, watching the beads of water form outside her glass.

"Revenge, life insurance, could be lots of motives. Besides, he said she threatened to kill him more than once."

"Did you find anything?"

"Yup. Her name ain't Kathy, it's Karen, with a K, and she owns a beauty salon. I found their weddin' announcement and then researched her name."

"You found out all that on your phone?" Impressive. How did they ever get anything done before the internet?

Pearl grinned. "Sure did." She clicked on an online link with her fingertip and held the phone up to her ear as it automatically dialed the salon's number. Sally watched as Pearl employed a stereotypical New Jersey accent and asked if Karen was cutting hair today. After a few minutes of listening to the one-way conversation, Pearl hung up, and her shoulders slumped.

"It ain't her," she said, slipping back into her southern accent. "She's been in the hospital the past week recoverin'. Complications from havin' her gallbladder removed."

Sally clucked her tongue. "That's awful. I hope she's okay."

Pearl shrugged and set her phone down. "It's a darn shame. I was sure it was her, but I guess she can't murder someone from a hospital bed." After a beat, she asked, "You hungry?"

Sally's stomach growled. "I am."

"Me too. All this detective work is taxin'." She slid off the stool and started walking.

They had been up well past midnight going over theories. She hopped off the stool and followed Pearl.

"What are you hankerin' for?" Pearl said, interrupting her thoughts.

"Oh, I don't know. You pick."

"How about seafood?"

"Perfect."

"Good. We can figure out our next suspect over shrimp so big that they beat up lobsters."

A few minutes later, they were settled at a table and holding glasses of white wine. "Do you remember the first time we shared a bottle of wine?" Pearl asked.

"Of course I do," Sally said, smiling.

It had been four years ago. Pearl had been facing a cancer

scare, which she'd only told Sally about because she had needed someone to drive her home from a surgical biopsy. After a long, tense week of waiting for results, she'd torn into the driveway in her convertible and beeped the horn. Sally had been in the middle of drying dishes. "What the heck," she'd mumbled, heading from the kitchen to the front room.

Pearl had beeped again, and Sally had opened the door. "What are you doing?"

"Get in, loser. We're fixin' to celebrate."

"Why are you calling me a loser?"

Pearl threw open the car door and hopped out. "I swear, don't you watch any movies?"

Sally had had no idea what she was talking about but she'd dried her hands and held up a finger. "Give me a minute. Harold is bowling tonight, and I was doing dishes."

"Hurry up. I got a bottle of wine and some good news."

Sally had smoothed her hair down and grabbed her purse. She'd scribbled a quick note to Harold before running out to the car. As she'd clicked her seat belt, she had tried to ask Pearl about the good news.

Pearl had just slid on her sunglasses and turned the radio up, singing along loudly as she'd driven down the street.

"Where are we going?" Sally had shouted over the music.

"To put our feet in the sand and celebrate life!"

Pearl had pulled into Island Lake State Park, sliding into a parking spot next to the water. The lot had been mostly empty in early September, with school already back in session. But it had still been hot, and the sun had been about an hour away from setting.

Sally had only come here a few times with the kids, and that had been years before. Why hadn't she come here more often?

She'd thought that it was a shame to live so close to the lake without ever taking advantage of it.

Pearl had grabbed a basket and blanket out of the trunk. Sally had slipped her shoes off and carried them pinched in her fingers as they made their way across the sand. They'd each held corners and spread the picnic blanket out before sitting. Sally had tried again to ask about the news, but Pearl had held up her finger. "Just wait."

She'd dug in the basket for a bottle of wine, an opener, and two plastic cups. Once the wine was open and Pearl had poured the glasses half full, she'd handed one to Sally. With an irrepressible grin, she had said, "Let's toast to me bein' cancer free and ready to live."

"Oh, Pearl, that is the best news ever." They had clinked glasses and drunk. Then Sally had thrown her arms around her friend and hugged her, tears of relief pricking her eyes. She hadn't realized how worried she had been until that moment.

They'd laughed and talked and watched the occasional couple wander down the beach holding hands or kissing in the glow of the sunset. Pearl had pulled out some cheese and fruit. How fancy, Sally had thought as she'd plopped a grape in her mouth. They'd spent the next hour watching the sunset and the stars come out, just waiting to be wished on.

That wine had been a sweet Riesling. This wine, which the waiter suggested as a favorite of the resort, was much drier. The waiter said it was a perfect pairing with fish. Sally preferred the sweet.

"I'm thinkin' we should look at Shannon and Ricky."

"Why?" Sally asked.

"You can't trust a woman who flaunts her boobs around in public."

"There's a big difference between going topless and murder."

Pearl narrowed her eyes. "Is there? Both would get you locked up where I'm from."

"True. And they were acting strange at the memorial service."

"Exactly. So here's the plan," Pearl said, picking up a shrimp and dipping it in cocktail sauce. "We are gonna pretend to be interested in their resort. Like maybe we will visit sometime and bring some friends. You know, lay it on thick." She waved her shrimp around as she talked, dripping sauce on the table.

"You think they will believe we want to go to a nudist resort?"

Pearl plopped the shrimp into her mouth and said, "Why not?"

"I'm not a woman who would ever go to a nudist resort."

Pearl took a long sip of wine. "But they don't know that."

"Oh, I don't know."

"Leave it up to me. I'll get to the bottom of this or die trying."

"Stop it. Don't joke about dying, not with poor Chuck." Her voice trailed off, and she put her hand on her chin. It was too sad for words.

"Oh my stars, I ain't jokin'. I am plannin' to do enough lyin' for both of us. And before you get all churchy on me, there are plenty of examples in the bible of people lyin' for a good reason. And findin' out who killed Chuck is a good reason."

"I know that," Sally said, irritated.

Pearl shifted in her seat. "Buckle up, because here they come now."

"Hello there," Shannon said. She was wearing a tie-dye t-shirt, the bottom half cut into fringe. Ricky's hands were shoved in the pockets of his jean shorts, and he wore a ball cap on his head that said *FBI*. Underneath, in smaller letters, it said *Female Body Inspector*.

"Oh, hi," Pearl said with a massive smile. "You guys already eat? If not, you should join us."

"Thanks, but we already ate." Shannon rubbed her stomach. "And I am stuffed. We had oysters, and you know what that means." She winked and wrapped an arm around Ricky's back. Ricky puffed his chest out like a peacock, ready to score.

Gross, Sally thought. She had never met people so open about their sex life. She knew far more about them than she ever wanted to.

"Oh darn," Pearl said, snapping her fingers, "I was hopin' you could tell us more about your resort. Sally here was askin' all sorts of questions." Pearl winked at Sally, who stared back in horror.

Shannon's face broke out into a grin, "Oh really? I knew you had a wild side," she said, shaking her finger at Sally.

"I don't...." Sally started to say but swallowed a grunt when Pearl kicked her under the table.

"What she means is that she doesn't know where to start. We should meet later, and you can tell her about it."
Ricky shifted his weight on his feet and nuzzled into Shannon's hair. "Come on, baby, we can talk business after we take care of business."

Shannon smacked his arm. "You are terrible." Then, turning back to Sally and Pearl, she continued, "Let's talk later. Unless you wanna join us now?"

Pearl laughed, but Sally shook her head and began to cough.

"I'm kiddin', sweetie. Although we could teach you a few things." With that, Ricky pulled her away from their table, and she turned back to give a quick wave, her other hand on Ricky's backside.

"Whew, those two are somethin' else," Pearl said when they were out of earshot.

31

Keep an Eye Out

On their way back to their room, they passed through the courtyard. Along one edge of the white stucco building was a conference center with exterior doors every few feet. One of the rooms was open, and Pearl paused in the doorway. The space was empty, but someone had spread out a stack of poster boards and set a box of markers on a table.

"What are you doing?" Sally asked.

"Keep an eye out." Pearl stepped across the threshold, leaned out of the doorway, and looked around. After making sure no one was around, she snuck into the room and grabbed a few of the boards and two markers.

When Sally met her with a stern look, Pearl said, "They were left over and just goin' to get thrown out, anyway. We got some real theories, and we need more than lipstick on a mirror." Pearl tried to look casual while holding the poster boards under her arm as they walked back to their room.

Pearl spent an hour transferring the information from the mirror to the boards. At her suggestion, Sally sketched a layout of the crime area.

"I knew it," Pearl said, "Face-up means he was pushed." She stepped back from the board and examined her list of suspects.

"That makes sense, but we don't know for sure," Sally said. There had been several cases she knew of where the victim was pushed down the stairs. It took more than just one piece of information to prove guilt.

Pearl looked up from her work. "We don't got proof yet. But we're gonna prove it was good old-fashioned murder."

"So, what's next?"

"We gotta get into Chuck's room. There are probably more clues there."

"How are we going to get in? It is taped off and probably locked."

"Not sure yet, but I'll think of somethin'."

"Maybe we could get housekeeping to let us in? Say we forgot something in there?" Sally said, shading in the bushes at the bottom of the stairs.

"Nah. They won't buy it. We gotta be more sneaky."

Sally stifled a yawn. It had been a long day. "I'm sure we can come up with something by tomorrow."

Pearl scoffed. "Tomorrow? We gotta do this tonight under cover of darkness." She pulled the poster board she was working on up off the small table and turned it to face Sally. "Here are our prime suspects. I added Karen and then crossed her off to keep our records straight."

Sally set the marker on the ground next to her and shifted onto her knees. "Tell me what you have so far."

Pearl's eyes lit up. "We know Karen didn't do it on account of her gallbladder poopin' out." She smacked her thigh, "See what I did there?"

Sally rolled her eyes. "Ha. Ha. What else do you have?"

Pearl was undeterred. "Okay, here's where it gets interestin'. We need more evidence, of course, but I narrowed it down to these people."

Besides Karen, the list contained Ricky, Shannon, Dottie, Mike, Juan, and someone labeled Unidentified Person.

"What's with the last one?" Sally asked.

Pearl looked at the board and replied, "Unidentified Person? Wanted to leave our options open till we get more evidence."

"More evidence?"

"From Chuck's room."

"You can't just break into his room," Sally said.

"You got a better idea?"

Sally paced between the beds. "No. But he's on the second floor. How will you even get in?"

Pearl smacked her knees and stood. "I got a plan."

Sally stopped pacing and looked at her friend. "Are you going to share it with me?"

Pearl stepped into the bathroom and grabbed her brush, pulling it through her hair. "I ain't got every detail worked out just yet. First, we gotta case the area."

Sally crossed the room and stood behind her in the mirror. "Okay."

Without pausing her brushing, Pearl said, "Let's go."

Sally rolled her eyes. "Are you sure we won't get into trouble?"

Setting her brush on the counter, Pearl leaned against it. "This ain't rocket science. We ain't settin' it on fire. We'll search his room and look for evidence. If we find nothin', I'll let it go, and we can move on. Cross my heart."

Sally tipped her head and raised her eyebrows.

"What? I promised." Pearl pulled her shirt over her head,

threw it on the bed, and grabbed a plain black shirt off the hanger. "I gotta blend in."

"I hope you're wearing clean underwear."

"Why?" Pearl asked, wrestling with the cotton to push her arm through the sleeve.

Sally pulled her bag up her arm. "In case you break your leg and need to go to the hospital."

Pearl clucked her tongue. "I ain't gonna break anythin'." She slipped a room key into her pocket and opened the door. "Come on."

Sally sighed. This was a terrible idea. Sally looked over at her suitcase in the corner, wanting nothing more than to pack it up and head back to the safety of her home. Instead, she followed Pearl out of the room and pulled the door closed behind her.

They tiptoed down the hall to Chuck's door. Pearl reached out and tried the handle while Sally scanned the area. Pearl mouthed, "locked" to Sally, who nodded in understanding.

A few minutes later, they were standing under the balcony of Chuck's room. Pearl was surveying the building. A tangle of trees hugged the side of the building. Pearl had one hand on her hip, and another shielded her eyes.

"I don't think there's anything we can do," Sally said. She nervously looked around.

Pearl had that determined glint in her eyes. She would not be deterred. Sally shifted uncomfortably on her feet as golf carts full of new arrivals passed by and couples headed out for a late show.

They were going to get into so much trouble. She would spend the rest of her life in a Mexican jail. At least then she would probably learn Spanish, Sally thought.

Sally and Pearl noticed the ladder at the same moment. It was a utility ladder leaning against the side of a building opposite the one they were trying to break into. Sally sucked in a breath, immediately visualizing Pearl falling backward to her death. Pearl didn't seem worried about death as a smile flashed across her face. She started toward the ladder, and Sally reached out to take her arm. Pearl looked up at her. "You got a better idea?"

Sally didn't have a better idea, so she dropped Pearl's hand and followed her to the ladder.

"You hold the ladder, and I'll climb and then let you in."

"Okay, but be careful."

Sally held the ladder as Pearl climbed. She silently prayed Pearl didn't fall to her death in front of her. At the top of the ladder, Pearl swung a leg over the balcony and then rolled over the rest of the way. She landed on the deck with a thump. Then she leaned over the railing and yelled, "Pull the ladder down, so no one sees. I'll meet you at the door."

32

How Embarrassing

Sally trudged up the stairs with a sense of dread. They had been using the other staircase since Chuck died. Her eyes instinctively scanned the railing and stairs for remnants of blood. Luckily it had been thoroughly cleaned. She wasn't sure which would be worse, finding something incriminating or not finding anything. Before she reached the landing, Pearl pulled open the door to Chuck's room with her mouth set in a satisfied smile. She waved Sally forward. Sally's gaze darted around. The coast was clear. There was no one in the immediate area. She ran her fingers across the stucco wall and crossed to the seafoam green door, which was open just wide enough to slip through sideways.

She pushed the door closed behind her and let her eyes adjust to the light of the one lamp Pearl had turned on after pulling the blackout curtains tight across the window. As the room came into focus, Sally sucked in a breath. One of the beds had been stripped. The mattress was hanging off the frame. The clothing previously strewn about the room was now piled on the second bed. The painting over the beds had been straightened, and the dresser drawers were closed.

"This is a crime scene. Should we touch anything?" Sally asked, tiptoeing across the floor towards the bathroom.

"It was ruled an accident, remember? Far as I can tell, that means we got free reign." Pearl used her legs to push the mattress back onto the bed frame. She searched behind the headboard and under the mattress. Sally copied her actions on the other bed. Once that was finished, they surveyed the room once more.

"I think we need to check pockets and under the bed. Don't forget between the cushions on the love seat," Sally said.

Pearl gave her a quick nod. "Makes sense to me."

They got to work. Each piece of clothing was searched and laid on the bed. Pearl groaned as she used a hanger to pick up a pair of boxer briefs. Sally covered her mouth with the back of her hand to stifle her laughter. Sally dropped to the floor and used her phone as a flashlight to scan under the bed. She fished out towels, socks, and other items. Then she noticed something pink. She couldn't tell what it was and had to lay flat on the floor to reach her hand out until her fingertips grazed the item and she could scoop it into her hand. She grunted as she withdrew her hand and opened it. It was a button. A hot pink button. She held it up. "Did you see a shirt this might belong to?"

Pearl squinted and then stepped closer to get a better look. "That looks like it's from a woman's shirt." She pulled back to meet Sally's gaze. "And who do we know that wears that color every day?"

They both said, "Dottie."

"What should we do with it?" Sally asked.

"Give it to me. I'll put it in my pocket."

Sally handed over the button, and Pearl slipped it into the pocket of her shorts and said, "Let's keep lookin'. We need to see if we can find the watch."

They split up again and resumed looking for anything suspicious. Sally headed towards the closet and spotted an emerald green box on the shelf. She balanced on her toes and reached to pull the box towards her. She recognized the luxury watch box's leather exterior, having once seen one at an estate sale. She carefully carried it to the dresser and set it down. Was the watch in the box? And if it wasn't, where was it? Lifting the lid, she ran her fingers over the smooth pale green suede inside. The box was empty. She closed her eyes and tipped her head back.

"What's wrong?" Pearl asked. Her head was deep in the bathroom vanity.

"Found the watch box, but not the watch."

Pearl sat back on her heels. "That ain't surprisin'." She grunted as she pulled herself up using the counter. "I'm gettin' too old for this."

Sally stood with her hands on her hips, not sure what to do next. They had the button. They knew the watch was missing. "Did you find anything?" she asked Pearl.

"Nope. Maybe we should look down again by where they found him. There could be somethin' in the bushes."

"Like what?"

"I don't know. But they're always findin' stuff in the bushes at murder scenes."

"Okay."

Pearl flicked off the lamp, and they both fumbled in the dark on the way to the door. Pearl put her ear to the door to ensure no one was in the hallway. Then she eased open the door and poked her head out.

"It's all clear," Pearl whispered.

Sally followed her out of the room and down the stairs. She pulled out her phone and flipped on the light. Pearl did the same, and they dug through the bushes for any evidence. They were leaning way over, butts in the air when they heard a voice behind them.

"You ladies okay?"

Sally struggled to extract herself from the bush and turned to see Juan grinning at her. He raised his eyebrows as she smoothed her hair, pulling a small stick out from the back of her hair. She cleared her throat. "Fine. Just looking for something." She flicked her wrist toward Pearl, still buried in the bush.

"Need some help?" he said, stepping toward the bush.

Sally put her arm out. "No, that's okay. We are just, um, looking for lizards."

Juan's eyebrows knitted together for a second. Then he shook his head and wagged his finger at her. "You stay out of trouble, okay?"

"Of course," Sally said, folding her arms and rocking on her heels.

Juan just shook his head again and kept walking.

Sally sighed. How embarrassing.

"Find anythin'?" Pearl asked, her voice muffled from the foliage.

Sally reached down into the bushes to push the branches aside. Her light reflected off something on the ground near the base of the plant. Flashing the light more, she could tell it was a cell phone. She reached down, trying to ignore the branches scratching her arm, and grabbed for it. "Think this is something?"

Pearl looked over. "That Chuck's phone? Give it here."

Sally held the phone solemnly in front of her and crossed the sidewalk.

"Does it work?" Pearl asked.

Sally pressed the button on the side, and she saw Pearl's face light up in the glow of the home screen. A photo of Chuck and what looked to be some professional cheerleaders stared back at them. Sally tried to open the messages, but it was locked. "Shoot. Any idea what his password could be?" She stared at the screen, waiting for Pearl to enter a code.

"No idea. Let's get back to the room and figure it out there." Pearl said, turning to head back up the stairs.

Back in the room, Sally lay on her bed and plugged the phone in to charge it. "Any thoughts on the password?"

Pearl stopped her pacing and looked up at the ceiling. "It could be anythin'. Try usin' password."

Sally frowned but tried the suggestion. She shook her head. "Even he isn't stupid enough to use that as a password."

"His cornbread ain't done in the middle."

"How are we going to get in?"

Pearl started pacing again. Sally could see her mind whirling. She snapped her fingers and grinned. "Flamingo Singles."

Sally laughed. "You're a genius."

Pearl pointed at the phone. "Better make sure it works before you hand out any awards."

When the phone lit up, Sally tried to enter the password. "It worked," she proclaimed, turning the screen for Dottie to see.

"I'm happier than a tornado in a trailer park right now," Pearl said, flopping on the bed next to Sally.

"What should I look for?"

"Text messages."

Sally opened the message tab and scrolled through. The last text messages were from Ricky. Sally pressed a finger to the conversation thread and read through it. Then she sucked in a breath. "Ricky threatened him."

"What? Where? Let me see." Sally handed Pearl the phone so that she could move the screen into range for her eyesight.

Ricky: Stay away from my wife
    Chuck: i can't help it if ur wife finds me $exy
    Ricky: You son of a bitch.
    Chuck: keep ur wife out of my pants :)
    Ricky: IF I CATCH YOU WITH HER, I WILL END YOU

As Pearl read the messages, her eyes grew wide. "Hot dog. Ricky threatened to kill Chuck, clear as day." She held the screen so they could both read.

Sally nodded. It looked like Ricky didn't appreciate that Chuck and Shannon had continued their relationship without his knowledge or participation. Pearl continued to scroll through the messages. Yikes. Sally did not need to know the rest of those details. She pushed the phone away as Pearl giggled and kept reading.

33

Such a Peach

Tuesday, October 19th

"Ricky is at the top of my list. We just gotta get him to spill the beans," Pearl said, unrolling her towel on a beach lounger. She was wearing her straw hat with the writing on it again.

"How are we supposed to do that?"

"Just be our charmin' selves and make Ricky and Shannon our new best friends." She sat down on the edge of the chair and pulled off her cover-up. Her black skirted bathing suit was cut low and had a wire that pushed her breasts up and in. She shimmied her shoulders.

Sally rolled her eyes. "You are going to make this weird, aren't you?"

Pearl batted her eyelashes. "Who, little old me?"

"Yes, you. I don't want to be dragged into some weird sexual situation. I'm warning you now, I will leave."

"Oh, lighten up. I'm gonna use my fabulous people skills and make 'em talk. Find out where they were and what they really thought about poor Chuck. I don't got the energy for any weird sex stuff, anyway."

Sally pulled the sunblock out of her bag and flipped the lid. She squirted a line down one arm and then the other, rubbing it in. "Okay, but you have to do the talking."

"You know, that travel website was lyin'. I ain't seen anyone named Sue or been offered drugs once," Pearl said, pulling off her lace swimsuit cover.

"I hope we don't interact with a drug dealer. That sounds awful."

"You don't gotta be in Mexico to meet a drug dealer. Heck, your neighbor could be one, and you'd never know."

Sally thought about her neighbors. Bob and Betty lived two doors down and had a rebellious kid who still lived in their basement at 23 yrs old. Pearl might be right.

"Next time we come here, we gotta go see the Aztec ruins. Been on my bucket list," Pearl said, swinging her legs onto the lounge chair.

"That sounds like fun," Sally said. She was glad they had kept this first trip simple, minus the murder, but she would be ready to venture out a little farther if they came back.

Sally and Pearl stayed on alert, and it wasn't very long before Shannon appeared. She was laughing, carrying a towel in over her arm in front of her concert t-shirt. Ricky walked next to her, wearing a Hawaiian print bucket hat and carrying a small cooler.

Pearl waved her hands wildly in the air. "Yew-hew, hello!"

Ricky noticed them first and poked Shannon in the arm. Shannon followed his gaze and then smiled, turning towards them. She stumbled in the sand and almost fell forward, grabbing Ricky's arm to steady herself. That led to another bout of laughter.

"Don't you two look cute," Shannon said, stumbling to a stop in front of them.

Pearl reached forward and threw her arms around Shannon. "You're such a peach."

Shannon grunted in surprise but returned the hug and picked Pearl up off her feet.

Ricky chuckled.

"Easy," Pearl said, "my bones are old. You'll break a rib."

Shannon set her down and beamed. "Are we friends now?"

Pearl let out a high-pitched laugh that made Sally snap her head towards Pearl in surprise.

"Of course we are," Pearl said, "In fact, we were just sayin' how we wanted to spend more time with you two. Minnesota ain't that far from Michigan."

Shannon clapped her hands and jumped up and down. She was not wearing a bra or a bathing suit top from the looks of it. Sally's suspicions were confirmed a few minutes later when she pulled her t-shirt over her head and revealed her very naked bosom.

Good grief. Why did Shannon have to be topless all the time? Was wearing a bathing suit top that big of a deal?

"We had so much fun last night that we slept through breakfast." Shannon wrapped her arm around Ricky and winked at Sally and Pearl.

Ricky dropped the cooler, took the towel down from over his shoulder, and laid it on a lounge chair. He picked up the towel Shannon had dropped on the sand and spread it next to his. As strange as their relationship was, it was clear that Ricky adored her.

Pearl kept her face neutral. "So what'd you guys get up to on Friday after we left? We heard things got wild."

Shannon licked her lips. "Really?"

Pearl nodded but kept silent.

"Hear that, Ricky? I told you we should have stayed. But no, you wanted to go back to the room."

"I had food poisoning and spent the night on the toilet. Remember?"

"You could have taken an antacid like I suggested."

"That wouldn't have fixed food poisoning. I had it coming out both ends." He looked at Sally and Pearl. "Pretty sure it was some bad seafood."

"Oh, I know. I had to listen to you moaning and puking all night. I could hardly hear my television show," Shannon said, a bite to her words.

Pearl reached over and elbowed Sally, speaking out of the side of her mouth. "Help me."

Sally nodded and watched Ricky and Shannon slather suntan oil on each other, waiting for an opening. She searched for something to say. "Um... so, tell us more about the Flamingo Singles. It seems like such a great group."

"Oh, it is," Shannon said, letting the bottle of oil drop back into her bag. She planted a quick kiss on Ricky and sank into her lounge chair. "We have made so many good friends. And Dottie runs a tight ship." She waved her finger in the air.

"That's one way to put it," Ricky said. He unzipped the cooler and pulled out a can of beer.

Shannon swatted his arm. "Oh, stop it." She turned back to Sally and Pearl. "She's just passionate, that's all. And she's having a rough time."

"Why?" Pearl asked.

"Because of Chuck. They used to be a thing. They tried to hide it, but everyone knew he adored her."

"While she was married?" Sally asked, trying to recall the conversations she'd had with Dottie.

"No. Only in the last year. Her old man was a deadbeat."

"What do you mean?" Sally brushed the sand off her feet. Dottie had said her husband had been a wealthy lawyer.

Shannon leaned in conspiratorially. "He was a big-shot lawyer just like Dottie likes to tell everyone. But he also had a gambling problem."

"Really?" Pearl asked casually, avoiding Sally's gaze.

"He left her penniless. She went from a country club Colonial to a two-bedroom condo."

"How terrible," Sally said and meant it. It was one thing to be in her shoes, where she might have to get a job after being widowed. It was another to have your whole life destroyed by a lying husband. No wonder she was working so hard for the Flamingo Singles.

"So she had to find a way to make money, and voila, the Flamingo Singles was born."

Pearl sat up. "Wait, I don't understand. How does she make money from the Flamingo Singles?"

Sally listened intently. When they'd shared fruit over breakfast, Dottie had alluded to other ways of supplementing her income, saying that what she made running the Flamingo Singles wasn't enough to live on. Did Ricky and Shannon know more?

Shannon lay back and closed her eyes. "It's not just her that makes money. It's all of us."

Ricky pulled his sunglasses halfway down his nose. "Shannon, maybe we shouldn't-"

Shannon cut him off. "Our new friends might be interested in making a little extra money, too. Right, girls?"

"Who doesn't want a little more jingle in their pocket?" Pearl said.

"What would we have to do?" Sally asked. Maybe this was an answer to her problems. If she could make money and travel, it would be perfect.

Shannon and Ricky shared a look. Shannon cleared her throat. "Chuck used to screen potential members. But, well, that isn't going to happen anymore." She choked on a sob. Ricky put his hand on her arm and whispered something to her. She nodded, wiped her eyes, and sniffed.

"I'm sorry. I just still can't believe Chuck is gone."

"So, who's gonna take his place?" Pearl asked.

"Dottie. She is the founder of the group anyway. Chuck had been co-leader for only a few months. They seemed to butt heads over stuff, and she was pretty mad at him the last time I saw them together."

Pearl swung her feet onto the ground in Shannon's direction, "What do you mean?"

"I don't know what they were fighting about that time. Chuck joined the group a year ago, and they started hooking up quickly. Then he started helping her with little things. She appreciated him, you know. But then they started to argue about money and stuff. It was rough at the end."

"Were they together Friday night? We saw Dottie at the bar, but not Chuck."

"Don't know," Ricky said.

"Oh, hey Mike," Shannon called out brightly.

Sally turned to see Mike walking towards them, his eyes on her.

34

That Escalated Quickly

"Hey, guys. Um, Sally, can I talk to you for a minute?" Mike pointed to the empty patio next to the beach.

"Sure," Sally said, getting up. She was glad he had found her. She needed to apologize.

They walked silently until they were out of earshot.

"I'm sorry," Mike said, raking a hand through his hair.

"Me too," Sally said, kicking a small rock into the bushes.

"I don't know why I acted that way. I was trying to be helpful, but I'm pretty sure I came across as a jerk." Mike shoved his hands into the pockets of his navy shorts and looked at the ground. "I just don't want you to get hurt."

Sally folded her arms in front of her, "You're not a jerk. I didn't react well either."

Mike looked up from under his lashes and smiled. "Truce?"

Sally dropped her arms to her sides and smiled, "Of course."

A smile on Mike's face reflected hers. "Good. I am supposed to meet some other Flamingos for a drink, but I will see you later."

Sally nodded, and they parted ways. She walked back to the

beach chairs, past a young couple sound asleep in a hammock hung between two trees. She smiled at their intertwined fingers, her heart lighter.

As soon as she reclined into her chair, Pearl leaned over Sally and scanned the area before saying in a low voice to Shannon and Ricky, "Do you think Chuck died by accident?"

Shannon and Ricky shared another look. "Why do you ask?" Ricky said in an even tone.

Pearl shrugged and fell back against her chair, "Just wonderin'. Seems unlikely that he would fall down the stairs face-up. If he fell, he would land face-down. You only land face-up if you got pushed."

"What?" Shannon asked.

"You didn't know? He was found face-up, which means he was probably pushed." Pearl stood up and demonstrated the difference between falling forward and being pushed backward. She flailed her arms and screamed as she pretended to tumble down stairs, displaying impressive dramatic skill.

Shannon stared at Pearl blankly. "I'm confused."

Good grief. What was there to be confused about? Sally thought Pearl did an excellent, albeit dramatic, demonstration of the difference.

Ricky cracked open another beer. "You think he was murdered?"

"I don't think. I know," Pearl said with a head nod.

"Oh my god, Chuck was murdered? By who?" Shannon's hand flew to her chest.

"Now that is the question, ain't it?" Pearl stood and stared at Shannon and Ricky.

Shannon hopped up, causing Sally to turn away until everything settled down. "Are you accusing us?"

"Of course not," Sally said.

"Unless you did it," Pearl added with a casual wrist flick.

Shannon scoffed. "You can't be serious." She and Pearl glared at each other. Sally wasn't sure what to do. She didn't dare to move.

Ricky stepped between them. "Now, ladies, I like nothing more than two girls going at it, but this isn't the time or place." He turned from Shannon's chair to face Pearl. "We had nothing to do with Chuck's death. I was on the bathroom floor all night, and Shannon had to bring me vodka every twenty minutes all night long."

Sally had to know. "I'm sorry. Did you say vodka?"

Ricky looked down at Sally. "That's right. I needed to stay hydrated."

"I can't believe this," Shannon exclaimed, throwing her hands in the air.

"Just what made you think we could do something like that?" Ricky asked, stepping behind Shannon and rubbing her shoulders.

"Yeah, I thought we were friends," Shannon pouted.

"We are friends," Sally said, patting Shannon's knee.

Ricky stepped around Shannon and lowered himself into a chair. "It was probably a robbery gone wrong or something. He was always flashing that gold watch of his. It's like a fishing lure for criminals."

Shannon nodded.

Pearl paced. "His watch?" She turned to Sally. "Did that housekeeper say he was wearin' his watch when she found him?"

Sally licked her lips. "No. She said he was wearing a gold necklace and ring, but no watch."

Ricky puffed out his chest. "Well, there you have it. He never took that watch off, not even to sleep or shower." Again Shannon nodded in agreement.

This was a new development. If Ricky and Shannon were guilty, why would they offer that critical piece of information, consistent with what Chuck himself had said to Sally and Pearl? Or were they trying to distract them? Either way, if they were guilty, they weren't going to admit it today. Sally cleared her throat and stood to pull Pearl to her, putting her arm around her shoulder, "We didn't think you were responsible. We hoped you knew something that would lead to the real killer."

Shannon reached up and took Pearl's hand. "Sorry I overreacted. It's been a long week, and I need a margarita."

"We are sorry for doubting you, aren't we, Pearl?" Sally squeezed her shoulder and let her nails dig in until she mumbled her agreement.

Pearl shook her arm off and grumbled as she walked back to her lounger. She started packing up her beach towel into her bag.

Sally watched. "What are you doing?"

"I am starvin', and we gotta find another suspect. Let's go drop our towels off in the room."

"Sorry," Sally said to Shannon and Ricky. Then she packed up her things and followed Pearl.

Back in the room, Pearl paced before her list of suspects. The last thing Sally wanted to do was follow her into more confrontations like the one they had with Ricky and Shannon. They needed to be strategic and subtle. Pearl was a bull in a china shop.

She glanced over at the morning resort letter. "Let's go do something fun. How about line dancing? That could be fun."

"Line dancing? So we abandon the hunt for Chuck's killer and selfishly have fun?"

Sally stomped her foot. "Yes. I want to have fun."

Pearl pulled her chin into her neck. "Did you just stomp your foot?"

Sally ran her fingers through her hair and rolled her shoulders back, "Yes. And I meant it." Her feet felt numb, and she was sure her tongue was swelling.

"Fine. If you feel that strongly about it." Pearl poked her in the chest. "But I am goin' to keep searchin' for clues."

Sally swallowed hard and nodded.

"Let's go for a walk and grab some lunch. Then we can go dance."

35

Nudists Next Door

"Maybe we'll run into that housekeeper again and we can ask her some more questions," Pearl said as they headed to a side of the resort they hadn't explored yet. As they walked, they took turns pointing out iguanas and a small animal that looked like a raccoon but wasn't. Sally was hoping to see a Mexican spider monkey, but they'd had no luck.

Passing through the central courtyard and by the restaurant, they wandered into a less populated area. "What would old Harold have thought about you drinkin' and carousin'?" Pearl asked and shot her a sideways smile.

Sally sighed, "He probably would've fallen out of his chair." She laughed. "He might have loved it." When they'd first met, she had been a free spirit ready to embrace life. He had been this strong, solid force to hold her feet to the ground and keep her from floating away. She smiled at the memory. It was the first time she'd thought of Harold without pain searing her heart.

Pearl looped her arm through Sally's as they walked. The buildings were closer to the resort's edge, and the doors were blue. A middle-aged woman came out of one of the doors wearing a maid's uniform. Taking a left turn just past an open door leading to a steamy laundry room with rows of industrial washers and dryers, Pearl slowed her pace and went uncharacteristically quiet.

"What?" Sally asked.

"Hush," Pearl said before tiptoeing across the grass between the sidewalk and a large wooden privacy fence.

"What are you doing?" Sally whispered.

Pearl waved her over and turned to peek between the fence slats. On the other side of the fence was the pool for the neighboring resort. Sally gasped. There were people just walking around, completely naked. And it didn't seem to matter how old they were or if they looked good naked. Nobody seemed to care. A heavy-set man floated in a bright pink ring. Luckily the tube had him folded in half, hiding his genitals. Sally stifled a giggle and looked at Pearl, then they both burst out laughing.

"Shhh..." Pearl admonished. "We don't need them hearin' us. They might make us join."

Sally didn't generally consider herself a prude. She watched R-rated movies and read some salacious drugstore paperbacks, but this was something else. She couldn't imagine walking around nude for all the world to see. "Have you ever been to a nudist resort?"

Pearl kept watching through the fence. "No, but I been to a topless beach. My husband and I used to travel and spent a fair amount of time on clothin'-optional beaches. He was a real stunner." She turned her head and winked.

When Sally dared to look again, a woman about their age was walking along the edge of the pool with a mimosa in her hand

and a wide-brimmed straw hat on her head. She smiled and waved at a couple lying in the sun. "Look at her, just hanging out there for the world to see. I can't imagine."

Pearl pointed to a different spot in the fence. "Look over there. That Dottie?"

Sally squinted till she spied the woman in a hot pink bathing suit leaning in and talking to two men. "It sure is. What is she doing over there? I thought you had to be a registered guest to get in."

"Don't know. But at least she ain't naked. My eyes are already burnin' from all that pale exposed flesh."

"Maybe she does business with them too?" Sally asked.

Pearl shook her head. "She don't seem like the nudist type. And those guys look familiar."

Sally squinted. "Look at their crocodile boots. They look like the cops that showed up at our door."

"And they ain't even nude. I knew they looked suspicious," Pearl said, nodding. "Why would they be at a nudist resort with Dottie?"

"I am sure there's a perfectly reasonable explanation for all of this," Sally said, although her mouth went dry, and she tugged at the hem of her shirt.

One of the men pushed his suit coat back to reveal a pistol strapped to his side. Sally sucked in a breath. But before she could say anything, Pearl waved her hands wildly over the fence, "Yew-hew, Dottie. Come have lunch with us."

Dottie turned towards the fence and shielded her eyes to see who was calling her name. The men started to fidget and look around. Dottie said something to them, turned on her heel, and headed to where the girls were waiting.

"Why did you do that?" Sally hissed. "She looks mad."

"Why would she be mad? I'm just bein' nice."

"I don't know, but she looks angry."

Dottie zeroed in on them, and her face changed when she was almost to the fence. She smiled and said, "Oh ladies, what are you doing spying on these fine people? Trying to get a sneak peek at some older gentleman?" She winked.

Pearl cleared her throat. "Oh, my stars. The last thing I need to see is a shriveled-up old man."

Dottie folded her arms. "Then what are you doing here?" Her smile was strained.

Sally put a hand on Pearl's arm to silence her. "We were just curious. I don't travel much and wasn't sure what a clothing-optional resort was all about." She forced a light tone. Why was Dottie being so weird about it? It's not like they had caught her nude. She didn't have any reason to be defensive.

Dottie paused to consider, and then her face relaxed, "Oh, that makes sense. You girls are so funny." She pointed down towards the beach. "There's a break in the fence down by the water. Meet me down there so I can cross back over, and we can go grab some lunch." Dottie headed towards the water.

Sally turned to follow her.

"If we have to eat with that woman, we're gonna get some information out of her."

Sally stopped. "Think you can get her to talk?"

"I sure do. She's been actin' jumpy as a cat in a room full of rockin' chairs. And who were those guys she was talkin' to?"

Sally remembered the pistol. "One of them had a gun."

"What? Are you sure?"

"Yes. He pulled back his jacket, and there it was, plain as day."

"Come on. We're goin' to find out what she had to do with

Chuck's death."

Pearl took off towards the beach. "Dottie, I wanna ask your opinion about somethin'."

Dottie carried her sandals in her hand. "Of course. What can I do for you?" She brushed a strand of blond hair out of her eyes.

Pearl scratched the back of her hand and said, "Well, I was thinkin'. If I wanted to join your Single Flamingo group, would there be a membership fee or initiation of some kind?"

Dottie looked from Pearl to Sally. "You're serious?"

"Of course," Pearl fawned, "We both wanna join, right Sally?" She kicked Sally's foot with the side of her heel.

Sally was watching Dottie for any signs of guilt. "Oh, yes, of course."

Dottie straightened her shoulders and set her jaw. Then she said, "If you are serious, we should talk about it. Our members are fiercely loyal and willing to do whatever it takes to protect the group."

"Protect the group from what, seagulls?" Pearl scoffed.

Dottie tapped her foot. "What do you mean? From anything. Danger, pain..."

"Why would they need protection?" Sally asked without thinking. What could the group be doing that would be dangerous? As far as they had seen, the group spent their time on the beach and at the bar and weren't in danger, except for poor Chuck. But they still didn't know what had happened to him.

Dottie's eyes darted between them. "You know that we work in international trade. And sometimes our work can be a bit risky." Her voice sounded hollow, and maybe there was something in her eyes. Fear? "But never mind. That is a discussion for another day." She waved them off and stepped down to the water, letting the waves wash over her toes. Then she turned back to them, all smiles. "I'm starved. Let's go eat." She pushed between Sally and Pearl, looped her arms through each of theirs, and started walking.

On the way to the restaurant, Dottie's phone started to ring. She fished it out of her bag and extended her arm to read the number calling. She frowned. "Shoot, I have to take this. Let's meet up later."

She waved goodbye and answered the call, holding the phone to her ear and whispering as she skittered away.

"That was rude," Pearl huffed.

"Should we follow her?" Sally said, keeping her eyes on Dottie just in case.

"Heck yeah."

Sally pointed in the direction Dottie had gone. "Maybe she's goin' back to meet with those guys."

They followed at a distance as Dottie retreated towards the nudist resort. They paused when they saw her stop in a nook of rooms and lean against the wall.

"Is she still on the phone?" Pearl asked, squinting.

"I don't think so." Dottie was standing in the shadows talking to someone Sally couldn't see, Dottie's phone hanging down at her side. Sally leaned forward and could make out the toes of crocodile boots. Why was she talking to the police officers again? "She's talking to those cops again."

Pearl scoffed, "If they are cops. We need to check into that for sure. Somethin' ain't right about them."

Dottie glanced their way, and Sally dropped down behind a bush. "Pearl, maybe we should leave."

"Yeah, this ain't gettin' us nowhere." Pearl shook her head

and looped her arm through Sally's. "Come on, Sherlock, let's go get some lunch."

Sally let Pearl lead her away but looked back over her shoulder. Dottie was staring after them, her jaw set and eyes narrowed.

36

Back Off

After lunch, Pearl suggested they sit down by the beach for a bit. Once they were settled, Pearl asked, "You sure the men Dottie was talkin' to were the same ones who were with the police when they found Chuck?"

Sally nodded. "Absolutely."

"Figures." Pearl leaned back in the Adirondack chair facing the volleyball court. "I'm more tired than a hooker on nickel Wednesday. Keep an eye out for Dottie." She let her eyes fall closed.

Sally pulled her paperback out of her bag, grateful for a few minutes to relax and read. After a few minutes, a shadow passed over her book, which she thought was a cloud crossing the sun, but it didn't move. She looked up. It was Dottie, hands on her hips, staring at her. She closed her book. "Um, hi."

"Why were you following me?"

Okay, so she was going to jump right in. Sally wasn't sure how to respond, so she reached over and patted Pearl's arm until she stirred and said, "What? Is it time for dinner?"

"Pearl, wake up," Sally said, pointing to Dottie.

"Yeah, wake up. I have some questions for you." Dottie kicked Pearl's foot with her strappy heel.

"Hey," Pearl protested, wiping her eyes and blinking rapidly until she focused on Dottie. "Get away from me."

"I will not. I want to know why you were following me."

Pearl dropped her head back and sighed. "The world don't revolve around you, Dottie."

"It doesn't revolve around you either, and I want answers."

Pearl smacked her hands against the arms of the chair and pushed herself up. "Maybe we were huntin' iguanas. Maybe we got lost. Why would we be followin' you?"

"I have no idea. You two are stalking me or something." Dottie looked at both of them. Sally sat, frozen. She wasn't sure what to say.

Pearl roared with laughter. "You think we would waste our time stalkin' you? What in the world for?"

Dottie crossed her arms and considered. "Maybe you're jealous or are trying to embarrass me. You've been acting strange ever since Chuck died."

Now Sally stood and joined Pearl. "And how did Chuck die, Dottie?" Sally asked, her voice steady as she met Dottie's gaze.

"You know more than you're tellin', and you ain't foolin' us by playin' dumb," Pearl said, feet set wide, finger poking Dottie in the chest.

Dottie sneered, "Listen here, you southern trash; I don't know what you're talking about."

Pearl huffed. "I see right through your fancy-pants façade. You better start talkin', 'cause I ain't backin' down."

Dottie clenched her fists at her sides and screeched in frustration. Then she turned on her heel and stomped away. After a few steps, she turned around and growled, "You have no idea who you're dealing with."

Pearl scoffed and turned to Sally. "I need a drink."

Not wanting to be left alone with Dottie, Sally followed Pearl as she headed to the pavilion bar and picked out a table that provided the best view of the foot traffic. "Someone's gonna slip up. All we gotta do is keep our eyes peeled."

"I'll grab drinks. The usual?" Sally asked.

Pearl nodded. When Sally returned, they nursed their drinks and leaned close to each other in order to recap everything they knew so far. After their glasses were emptied and they had compared notes, Pearl smoothed her hair. "I need another drink."

Sally stood to fetch it, happy for the chance to stretch her legs. She shifted her hips to drive out the stiffness while she waited for the bartender, who she didn't recognize. She caught his attention, and he danced over to take her order for two margaritas. While he prepared the drinks, Sally turned to scan the pavilion. Mike wasn't there. None of the Flamingo Singles were in the area. How strange, since at least one of them always seemed to be parked near the bar.

"I'll be right back," Sally said to the bartender. She headed to the restroom around the back of the pavilion.

When she returned, she was greeted by two bright pink margaritas with giant strawberry garnishes cut into flowers and balanced on the rims. "Thank you," she said, lifting the drinks. Then she noticed that one of the napkins the bartender had slipped under the glasses had writing on it. She set the drinks back down and lifted the napkin. A handwritten note was scrawled across the lime green paper, slightly damp from the condensation on the glass. Her breath caught as she read the words written in red.

Back off, or you're dead.

The threat was smeared from the ring of her drink, but still legible.

"What's takin' so long?" Pearl asked, sidling up beside her at the bar.

Sally couldn't speak, so she just pushed the note down the bar with the tip of one finger, wiping her hand on her shorts after.

"What's this?" Pearl asked, sliding on the readers dangling from a chain around her neck. After reading the message, she swore under her breath and looked at Sally.

Sally was pale. Her feet were numb. Was she having a heart attack? Great. She was probably going to have a heart attack in Mexico.

Pearl picked up the napkin and waved it around, Sally taking a step back to avoid touching it again. "Where'd this come from?"

"It was under my drink when I came back from the bathroom." Sally stared at the note while Pearl began to scan the room, eyes narrowed.

"Recognize the handwritin'?" Pearl asked.

Sally shook her head.

Pearl leaned over the bar and motioned to Juan, who hadn't been there earlier. "Hey, did you see who left this note?"

Juan sauntered over and frowned. "No, ma'am. I just got here."

Pearl huffed. "Who else was here?"

"Ricardo, but he's on break for one hour."

"Oh, my stars. Somebody must have seen somethin'."

"I don't know," he said with a weak smile. "Please, come back later." He turned his attention to a couple at the end of the bar.

"Come on," Pearl said, grabbing her drink. "We'll come back when Ricardo's done with his break."

Pearl was still ranting about the note when they opened the door to their room. Her mouth dropped open, and her purse slipped out of her hand when she saw the mirror over the dresser. Her pink lipstick list of suspects had been angrily smeared, some of the color dragged onto the wall next to the mirror and the top of the dresser. In its place were big black letters.

Go Home. We are not messing around.

Pearl and Sally stood in front of the message, faces ashen.

Sally wasn't sure what she was most upset about, the message or the fact that someone had been in their room. Tears sprang to her eyes, and her heart raced as she scanned the room for anything out of place or anyone who shouldn't be there. Sally moved cautiously to the bathroom and pushed the door open with her foot, stepping out of sight. The door hit the back wall, and a shampoo bottle fell off the shower shelf. Sally shrieked.

Pearl was there in a flash. "What was that?"

Sally laughed nervously. "Sorry, nothing." She shook her head, "I just knocked down the bottle." Sally pulled the door closed and turned back to the mirror. "Who did this?"

When Pearl didn't answer, Sally turned to her. "Pearl? Did you hear me? What's your theory?"

Pearl crumpled onto the bed and sighed. "No idea." Her face twisted, and she looked up at the ceiling.

What was wrong with her? Pearl took everything in stride. Maybe she was having a heart attack. Out of instinct, Sally grabbed Pearl's wrist to find her pulse.

"Oh my stars, what are you doin'?" Pearl shook Sally's hand loose.

"Are you having a heart attack or something?" Sally felt her forehead and leaned down to look into her eyes."

Pearl waved her arms in front of her. "Get off me. I'm fine."

Sally huffed and stepped back. "You scared me."

Pearl stood and brushed invisible lint off the front of her shirt. "I can't lose you too– I couldn't bear it."

"Why would you lose me?"

Pearl grabbed the note and waved it in Sally's face. "Did you not understand this? Someone is threatenin' you because of me."

Sally grabbed the note from her hand and crumpled it, then dropped it onto the floor.

"That don't change nothin'," Pearl said, crossing her arms in front of her.

The room began to blur, and Sally had to sit on the bed. She had no idea what to do. Pearl had always been the strong one in their friendship. She was brave, bold, and tenacious. When Pearl had shared the story of her children, Sally had understood. Then she'd signed on to this adventure with all her heart. How could Pearl be faltering, now?

Pearl sat next to her. "I don't want you to get hurt."

Sally looked at her. Pearl's brow furrowed, and she frowned. "I am not interested in getting hurt either, you know."

Pearl smiled palely. "Good. Then we agree. We're gonna back off and let it go." Pearl's eyes were conflicted. Full of fear, she grabbed Sally's hand and gripped it with white knuckles.

Sally stared at their hands. They had been through so much together. And she knew, without a doubt, that if Pearl let this go, she would regret it. Pearl couldn't stand injustice. She was

195

the first to step up when someone was wronged or in danger. She would put her life on the line without flinching. She was just scared.

Sally shook her head in disbelief. "We can't let it go."

"What do you not get?" Pearl said. Standing and flailing her arms, she continued. "They were in our room, Sally. They threatened us twice."

"Don't you think I know that? I'm not an idiot."

"I didn't say you were, but good gravy, this is serious."

Sally met her eyes with conviction. "I know that. And this means you were right. It wasn't an accident."

Pearl paced in front of her. "It don't matter anymore. I'm gonna get us a flight home."

As Pearl scanned the room looking for something, Sally turned to watch her. "What about Chuck?"

"What about him? I ain't puttin' you in danger for someone who got himself killed. We gotta go home." Pearl stomped over to scoop up her phone.

37

Hot Damn

While Pearl called the airline, Sally headed to the balcony to clear her head. They needed a plan. They weren't safe in their room, that was for sure. But she didn't want to go home. That would prove her son right, and then what? Stay in that house for the rest of her life? No. That wouldn't do.

A new room might help. Maybe they should talk to the resort security. But she wasn't sure security could be trusted. Someone in their ranks had ruled Chuck's death an accident. They may be in on it. No, it was better to handle this themselves. Too bad Pearl hadn't brought her gun. It would have been nice to be armed.

Inside her pocket, Sally's phone started ringing with the song she had assigned to her daughter. She fished it out and answered.

"Mom! How is the trip?"

Sally wasn't sure how to answer that question. The trip had been both glorious and terrifying. But she decided on the most prominent emotion. "Liberating."

"Really?"

"Strangely, yes."

"Are you looking forward to getting home?"

Sally thought about her little house with the sunflower kitchen and newly painted living room. As much as she longed for the security of her little home, she wasn't ready to leave. Sally wasn't scared, which surprised her. She was determined. "I miss you. But I'm not quite ready to go home yet."

"Good. Enjoy every minute."

"I will." She sat up and took a breath. "Thank you, Lauren, for always being such a wonderful daughter. I love you."

"I love you too, Mom." After a beat, Lauren continued. "Hey, I went through your finances like you asked. You won't be able to buy a sports car anytime soon, but you should have enough money to get by with Dad's pension and investments."

"Thank you for doing that. It is such a relief."

"Good. I can't wait to hear all about your trip. Make sure you stay out of trouble."

"Of course. Just a boring vacation for two old ladies," Sally chuckled.

"Hey, I need to grab the kid from daycare. I'll see you when you get back."

When she hung up, Sally sat with her hands folded across her knees, staring at the sea. Her mind raced with thoughts of Harold, Chuck, and whoever it was that had threatened them. Logically she knew they should leave. She had always run away from danger while Pearl insisted on running towards it, and if Pearl was the one saying that they should leave...

Pearl slid open the door. "That was a bust. We can't get an early flight home without payin' out the nose." She closed the slider behind her, flopped into the chair next to Sally, and tipped her head back, eyes closed.

"Good. I don't want to go home early," Sally said quietly.

Pearl turned to Sally. "Didn't we both wanna hightail it out of here?"

"No. We have come this far and are obviously on the right track." Sally motioned around the room. "Or they wouldn't have tried to scare us."

Pearl smacked her thighs. "Hot damn. We're really gonna solve this case?"

"We should change rooms, though. This one gives me the creeps."

"You ain't lyin'. I'll call the desk and make it happen. Maybe tell them we saw a spider or somethin'." Pearl pushed herself up from the chair and returned to the room to make the phone call.

Sally bowed her head. She hadn't prayed much since Harold died, but this seemed like the right time to seek God. She was thankful for how far she had come and for all the joy they had experienced on the trip. She loved Pearl and was grateful for her friendship. They needed protection. Hopefully, God could help keep them safe. She sat in silence until peace washed over her.

The fear in her mind was chased away by quiet determination. This was her life. She finally had the chance to do everything she'd always wanted and she wouldn't let anyone take that away from her. This was her vacation. Pearl was right about Chuck having been murdered, and he didn't deserve to have his killer go free. Pearl had been so strong for her over the years, and now it was her turn to be strong for Pearl.

She stood with purpose and headed to the bathroom, passing Pearl, who was heading to the balcony. After pulling out her makeup remover, Sally grabbed a wash cloth and crossed to the mirror. A flash of anger fueled her as she furiously scrubbed the mirror clean. The lipstick and eyeliner smeared more before she folded the washcloth and started again. With each swipe, her image in the mirror became clearer. When she finally stood before the mirror, she saw herself in a new light. Her face was flushed, sweat dripping down her hairline. But her eyes were clear. For the first time in years, she felt strong.

Pearl pulled the slider shut and announced triumphantly, "We got ourselves a new room. It'll be ready in an hour."

"Good job," Sally said and smiled thinly. "I will talk to Juan. I want to see if he knows anything else about who may have threatened me."

"I'll come with you," Pearl said, throwing her suitcase onto her bed. "We can pack up when we get back."

Sally shook her head. "No. If we both go, he might be less likely to talk. Let me see if I can get some information out of him."

"That ain't safe."

Sally was sick of being afraid. She'd spent her whole life trying to stay safe and had still ended up in this mess. "Let me do this, Pearl. I need to do this."

Pearl tipped her head and narrowed her eyes. "Who are you, and what have you done with Sally?"

Sally nodded and swallowed. Suddenly her bravado faltered. Someone out there had threatened her. They had been in their room. What if she ran into them outside? No, she thought. She could do this; she had to do this for Pearl.

"All right then." Pearl crossed the room and patted her back. "I'm proud of you. Go get 'em."

Sally couldn't back down now. Gathering the embers of courage still burning in her heart, she slipped her purse over her shoulder and headed for the door. She would be fine. Someone was just trying to scare them. She grabbed the knob and pulled the door open. Looking back, Sally saw Pearl watching her with a broad smile.

Descending the stairs, Sally pictured where Chuck had fallen. What had happened to his luxury watch? Did someone steal it? That would have to be figured out later. For now, she needed to find out who had written that note. She had a future to enjoy, and no one could threaten her and get away with it. She straightened her shoulders and headed to the pavilion bar.

Only a few guests were scattered among the tables, and she was glad that no one from the Flamingo Singles was there.

"I'll take a frozen daiquiri," she said to Juan.

He smiled broadly at her. "Of course, *señorita*."

Sally slipped onto a bar stool and set her bag on the bar next to her. Wasn't *señorita* the title for a young, unmarried woman? Maybe he was just trying to butter her up.

A moment later, Juan set a napkin down and presented a daiquiri with a tall garnish of pineapple and cherries. "*Gracias*," Sally said, smiling.

"For you, *señorita*, anything," he winked.

Sally sipped the drink and immediately got an ice headache. Shaking her head, she waited for the feeling to pass. Then she watched Juan, who was rinsing and drying margarita glasses. He occasionally paused to serve someone a cold beer or mixed drink. Juan was here every day. He must have seen something.

"Juan, can I ask you a question?"

Walking over, he dried his hands. "Of course."

She smiled and leaned in. "Someone left a note for me earlier, at about 5:00. The note was more of a threat."

Juan's eyes widened. "A threat?"

Sally nodded. "Did you see anyone around that time who was acting strange?"

Juan put his hands on the counter and leaned his head back, thinking.

Sally leaned forward again. "I mean, anyone acting suspicious, asking for a pen, anything like that?"

Juan leaned forward and whispered, "No one should threaten you. I wasn't working that time, but I did hear from Ricardo that someone tipped him extra to put a note under someone's glass. He didn't tell me what it said, just gloated about his tip."

Sally's breath caught in her throat. "Who was it?"

Juan picked up a glass and started drying again as if buying himself time.

"Please, you have to tell me. I won't say anything about where I found out. But I could be in danger, and if you know something, you have to tell me."

Juan sighed. "It was Miss Dottie."

"Are you sure?" Sally's mouth went dry.

Juan nodded gravely. "Please, I don't want any trouble." Juan looked around to ensure no one was listening to their conversation. "I need this job."

"Of course. Thank you, Juan."

Sally sat back on her heels. She needed to go. Pearl would know what to do next. Dottie couldn't just get away free and clear. She didn't get to threaten people, be a bully, and who knew what else.

That night they settled into their new room on the other side of the resort, far away from Dottie and her crew. It didn't face the ocean, but at least it was on the ground floor, and they felt safe.

Pearl wanted to confront Dottie immediately, but Sally

convinced her that they needed a plan. Dottie wasn't going anywhere, after all.

"I knew that woman was one doughnut short of a dozen. She's up to no good," Pearl said, unzipping her suitcase.

Sally eyed her. "You did? You didn't say anything."

Pearl waved her off. "You wouldn't have believed me. You were ready to paint yourself pink and stand on one leg to be one of the Single Flamingos."

Sally pursed her lips. "That's not true. I just thought the group looked fun." She shrugged and pulled open the dresser drawer to carefully place her folded pajamas inside.

"Remind me to add crocodile boots to the evidence list. Good on you for noticin' that."

Later, Sally lay in bed, steeling herself to confront their bully. How would Dottie react? She didn't seem like the type to throw punches. But her nails were filed into efficient weapons if she chose to use them. Sally had no idea what they would do if it came to that. When she finally drifted off, she had a nightmare about Dottie pinning her to the ground and pulling out clumps of her hair while Pearl stood by, laughing.

38

Now What?

Wednesday, October 20th

The following day Sally tried to shake off the dream as the hot shower poured over her body. For years she had escaped into the shower for a few minutes of peace while three children ran around playing cops and robbers, or fighting over some small toy that had been promoted from "forgotten" to "suddenly significant and in-demand."

A loud knock on the door echoed through the bathroom, and Sally turned off the water. "Yes?" she called out.

"Breakfast is here," Pearl replied.

Sally stepped out of the shower and quickly dried off, wrapping her hair in the towel and throwing on her robe.

Plates of eggs and slices of perfectly-cooked bacon sat on a linen-covered cart brought to their room. Pearl had insisted that they order room service. Sally had protested at first, since it was an extravagance that seemed unnecessary. But Pearl had reminded her that they needed to stay out of sight until they were ready to confront Dottie on their terms. It was the fanciest thing Sally had ever done, and she smiled as she sat in one of the chairs that Sally had pushed up next to the cart.

"Are you sure we shouldn't go to the police?" Sally asked Pearl, who was lifting little jars from a basket on the cart and reading the labels before selecting the strawberry preserves.

"You know we can't do that," Pearl answered, twisting the lid until it popped and the seal broke. "Not without some solid proof to show them."

"How are we going to get proof?"

Pearl grabbed her cell phone from the bed and held it up, shaking it. "This little puppy is gonna help. We'll record our conversation with Dottie and get her to confess."

"It can't be that simple."

Pearl shrugged. "Maybe not. But it's a place to start."

Sally savored the buttery eggs and bacon. There was little chance Dottie was going to offer up a confession. They would have at least some solid evidence if they could find Chuck's luxury watch. And if Dottie had pushed him down the stairs, maybe she had taken it. "We need to search her room."

Pearl held her fork, suspended between her plate and her mouth. "What?"

Sally cleared her throat. "We need to search her room. We know there was a pink button in Chuck's room. If we can find the shirt it came from, that might be enough for the police to question her again. We also know his watch was missing when they found him. What if it's in her room?"

Pearl set her fork down and narrowed her eyes, swallowing a smile. "Are you, my sweet, sweet Sally, suggestin' we break the law?"

Sally waved her off. "Oh, stop it. We crossed that bridge ages ago."

Pearl nodded and resumed her eating. Sally continued. "She bragged about never missing water aerobics with Juan. It starts..." she grabbed the schedule off the dresser and scanned the list of events, "...in an hour."

"Sounds like a plan," Pearl said between bites. "Seein' Juan in his little glitter shorts is the cherry on top."

They finished eating and pushed the cart into the hallway for the staff to retrieve.

"Let's take it slow and make sure she's gone. With our luck, this'd be the one mornin' she was too hungover to samba in her bikini," Pearl said as they worked their way towards Dottie's room. They stopped at the end of her building and watched as Dottie closed the door to her ground-floor room and strolled towards the pool in her bright pink swimsuit, a pink and black flamingo print sarong wrapped low on her hips.

"Try the front door first," Pearl said.

"It locks automatically," Sally replied.

"Maybe she left it open."

They sauntered causally over to her door and tried the handle. Locked. "Round back," Pearl whispered.

They made their way around the building, the bushes between the sidewalk and patio scratching their skin. Sally kept watching while Pearl pulled on the slider. Locked.

"Damn."

"What now?" Sally asked.

Pearl stepped back from the slider, her hands on her hips. "Look," Pearl said, pointing to the open bathroom window to the right of the sliding door.

Sally folded her arms and tried to calculate how and, more importantly, if they could climb through that window. It might work.

"Gimme a boost," Pearl said, positioning herself below the window and grabbing the sill.

"Are you sure about this?" Sally asked. The last thing Sally needed right now was to throw out her back trying to push Pearl through a window.

Pearl turned back to Sally. "Of course I'm sure. Now boost me up." She lifted a leg and wiggled her foot for Sally to grab and lift.

Sally blew her bangs out of her face and bent over to cup her fingers under Pearl's foot. She bent her knees to lift with her legs. She took a deep breath and heaved.

"Oof," Pearl said. "Higher."

"I can't lift any higher," Sally said. She wasn't sure how much longer she could hold her. There had to be another way. In the corner of the patio was a plastic chair designed to look like rattan. Maybe they could use that. And Sally was taller, so it would be easier for her. "I'm going to let you down. There's a better way," she said, carefully lowering Pearl back onto the patio.

Pearl grunted and stood up, straightening her clothing. "Thought I was goin' to end up stuck in that window 'til the end of time."

Sally grabbed the chair and dragged it over to the window. She stood on the seat and peered into the bathroom. The window was positioned over the counter. At least she wouldn't have to contend with a sink or toilet. "I've got this. Stay back and keep an eye out." She pulled herself up through the window, her arms grabbing the end of the counter as she struggled to turn her body. She was almost through when she paused. Now what? She was hanging out of a window, feet in the air, and needed to land without breaking her neck. She twisted and shimmied her rear through the frame, landing in a fetal position on the counter. Then she pulled herself up onto her elbows and hands, swung her feet over the counter's edge, and hopped down onto her feet. She stood for a second, evaluating herself for pain and injury. Surprisingly, she was okay.

"You alive?" Pearl asked through the window.

"Yes," Sally answered, brushing the dust off her shorts. "Meet me at the slider."

39

Eureka!

Sally turned, slid the window shut, exited the bathroom, and rounded the corner to the slider. After flipping the lock, she pulled open the door. "We did it," she said, beaming.

Pearl shook her head. "Ain't you the cat's meow? Can't believe you did that." Then she laughed. "You shoulda seen your butt in the air and your feet stickin' out like a bucket of fried chicken." She wiped her eyes. "Shoulda got a video." She smacked her knee and pushed in past Sally, who was glad Pearl didn't have a video.

They stood in the middle of Dottie's salmon-colored room, the crisp white bedding ruffled from the night before. Pink designer clothing was carefully hung in the closet. A variety of shoes was lined up along the bottom of the closet.

"Where do we start?" Sally asked. She scanned the room, looking for anything out of place. What did they expect to find?

"You take the closet. I'll get the dresser. Then we can check the beds and nightstands. She might have put somethin' between the mattresses or under her pillow."

"Okay," Sally said, moving to the closet. Dottie's clothes

were beautiful. She could have used some color variation, but the stitching and fabrics were top quality. She let the silk of the pale pink blouse side through her fingers. The shirt must have cost hundreds of dollars. How could she make that much money? She checked the pockets of each item. The only things she found were a small white sea shell and a five-dollar bill.

Reaching deep into the closet, she pulled out a hot pink blazer with 3/4 cuffed sleeves. The lining was black with little pink flamingos. She checked the pockets and noticed the pink threads on the front, sticking out of the fabric from where a button should be. "Hey, I found something." She held the blazer up and pointed to the frayed threads near the collar.

Pearl pulled her head out of the dresser drawer she was rummaging through, bras in both hands. "What?"

Sally bit back a laugh and shook the blazer. "Notice anything missing?"

Pearl squinted. "Button?"

Sally nodded triumphantly.

"Good find." Pearl pointed to the closet. "But put it back, so she don't know we know."

Sally turned to slide the hanger back down the rack.

"Wait, you should take a picture of it with your phone. We might need it later."

That was a great idea. Sally pulled her phone out of her pocket and held the hanger in one hand while she snapped a photo with the other. After she put the blazer back, she moved on to the bottom of the closet. She checked all the shoes and noticed Dottie's suitcase tucked in the back. She reached for it, pulling the suitcase out.

"Eureka!" Pearl called out by the dresser.

Sally abandoned the suitcase and turned to see what Pearl

had found.

"Lookie here," Pearl said. She was pulling something out of the drawer. It flashed in the light, the gold band reflecting the ray of sunlight cutting across the floor. Pearl turned towards Sally and held it on her finger, letting it swing with a hypnotic rhythm.

Sally's jaw dropped. The luxury watch. This was actual evidence connecting Dottie to Chuck's death. Pearl nodded, her grin almost manic. "We got her." She slid the watch into her pocket and moved to the next drawer.

"What now?" Sally said, subconsciously moving towards the slider.

"Whoa, we ain't done yet."

"Oh," Sally replied, a little disappointed. She glanced down at her phone; they didn't have much time. Then she remembered the suitcase and stepped back towards the closet, leaning in and grabbing the luggage's handle. She was surprised to find it was heavy. She used both hands to heave it onto the bed with a whoosh of air.

"Oh my stars, what's in that thing?" Pearl asked, abandoning the open drawer and stepping next to Sally. Sally stood with her hands on her hips. What did she have in there? Did they even want to know? Visions of tense scenes set to dramatic music from all the murder mystery shows she had watched flashed through her mind, pausing on moments of truth where unzipping or pushing various containers open revealed horrific discoveries. Was she ready for that?

Before she could decide, Pearl leaned over and unceremoniously pulled the zipper around the case, snagging it on the lining and having to yank it to break it free. When the zipper was resting at the end of the track, Pearl paused, too. The room was heavy with anticipation. Whatever was in this suitcase was important, Sally was sure of it. She turned to Pearl.

"Well, it's now or never," Pearl said. She used two fingers to hook the top of the case and threw her hand up to send the lid flying backward.

Neither of them said anything. Sally tipped her head to the side and bit her lip, giving her eyes and brain time to process what she saw. "Is that..." she started.

"Yup," Pearl replied. The suitcase contained four blocks of white powder in clear plastic bags with packing tape around the edges. Sally froze, her voice caught in her throat. Pearl began to dance a jig.

Sally turned to her friend, who was laughing as she danced. She was actually losing her mind this time. "What is wrong with you?" Sally asked as she stared at the open suitcase. Drugs. Real illegal drugs. Was this what they had been smuggling in to "help" people? Were all the Flamingo Singles in on it? Sally took a step back from the bed.

"Don't you get it? We were right. Dottie is a drug mule and probably a murderer. Now we got proof." Pearl grabbed Dottie's brush off the nightstand and poked at the plastic wrapping as if it were a dangerous snake waiting to strike.

A wave of panic swept over Sally. She grabbed the top of the suitcase and slammed it down, pulling the zipper haphazardly around the track. Then she lifted the case and moved the shoes out of the way with her foot so she could push the drug-filled suitcase back into the back of the closet. She bent over, straightened the shoes, and then let out a breath as she stood. Dottie had great taste, even if she wore too much pink. Sally brushed her fingers along the luxury fabrics of the tops and skirts one more time.

"You plannin' to steal some of those clothes?" Pearl asked. "If not, let's get out of here."

40

Here's a Secret

"Let's leave the door unlocked. Dottie will think she did it by mistake," Pearl theorized, pointing to the bathroom window.

"I hope so. I'm not going back through the window again, especially with only concrete on the other side to catch me if I fall." Sally pulled open the slider and was blasted by the hot wind off the ocean.

Pearl scoffed. "You don't think I could catch you? I was a lifeguard, you know."

"In the early 1970s?" Sally pulled the door shut behind them and wiped her hands on her pants.

Pearl seemed to be doing mental math in her head. "Yeah, but I'm sure it's like ridin' a bike. Anyway, don't matter now."

"Do you think Juan could help us find someone in the police department that can we can talk to?" Sally liked Juan. He had told her about Dottie, and she trusted him. And no, she told herself, it wasn't just because he flirted with her relentlessly.

"Ain't no time. We gotta find Dottie and confront her."

Sally's eyebrows knitted together. "Are you sure that's a good idea?"

"I wanna see her squirm. And what's she gonna do, shoot us?" Pearl looped her arm through Sally's and said, "Let's go find some lunch. We can carb load for the big shakedown."

They had only taken a few steps when a voice sounded behind them shouting, "Hey!"

They whirled around. Standing on the sidewalk, her eyes narrowed in confusion, was Dottie. "What in the world were you doing in my room?"

Sally's breath caught in her throat. Pearl stood her ground. "We know what you did."

Dottie looked at Sally and then back at Pearl. "I'm sorry. I have no idea what you are talking about."

"You killed Chuck," Pearl said through gritted teeth.

Dottie's hand flew to her neck and she focused on Sally. "How could you accuse me of something so awful?"

Sally swallowed and opened her mouth to speak. Pearl touched her arm and said, "Dottie, we may not know why you did it, but we know you are responsible. And you're not going to get away with it."

Dottie fidgeted with her room key and eyed Pearl. Sally leaned against the wall, fearing she might pass out. After what seemed like hours, Dottie dropped her hands to her sides and threw her head back. "Oh, fine, you win."

"What?" Pearl asked.

Dottie took a step forward. "You figured it out. Yes, I did it. But you have no idea how hard I work to keep all this going."

Sally wasn't sure she had heard right. Did Dottie just admit to murder?

"What are you going to do about it? Nobody is going to miss Chuck. And even if you tell, who will they believe, you or me? *I* am a respected tour operator bringing in thousands of

215

business dollars. Here's a secret." She leaned in and cupped her mouth with her hands." I'm untouchable." She leaned back and crossed her arms. "You should have minded your business. Now, what are you going to do?"

Pearl balled her fists. "We're gonna make sure you don't get away with this. And I got proof." She fished the gold watch out of her pocket and held it up.

Fear flashed in Dottie's eyes. "Where did you get that?"

"From your room. And ain't you missin' a pink button? We found it in Chuck's room. We've got you."

Dottie's face was crimson as she lunged for the watch. Pearl sidestepped her, causing her to stumble forward, and quickly turned to Sally. "Come on."

Dottie found her footing, whirled around, and tried to grab Pearl again. Sally stepped between Dottie's feet. Dottie tripped on Sally's ankle, then went down with a smack on the cement. Pearl swung around. "Nice job."

Dottie swore and tried to get up, her knees bloody and hands scraped. Sally ran past her and followed Pearl. Dottie's shrieking voice trailed after them, "You can't prove anything!"

41

.

On the Run

Sally's heart pounded in her ears. She had been a runner in high school, but that had been a long time ago. Dottie's voice followed them, yelling for them to stop.

"What the hell is wrong with that woman?" Pearl panted. "Is she still chasin' us?"

Sally turned her head quickly and caught sight of Dottie's hot pink bathing suit weaving between people in the crowded courtyard. "Yup."

"That woman is one number short of a bingo," Pearl said.

Sally agreed. Dottie was a couple of years older than they were, but for some reason, she was faster and gaining on them. "We need to do something," Sally huffed. There was no way they could outrun Dottie.

"I got an idea," Pearl said, taking a sharp left between two buildings.

Sally followed, having no idea where they were going. Ahead, blocking the sidewalk, was a golf cart. Eddie, of the kayak adventure, was carrying suitcases up the stairs for a couple waiting by an open room door. Pearl jumped in the driver's seat of the cart. Sally skidded to a stop. "What are you doing?"

"Gettin' us out of here. Now hop in."

Sally looked back to where they had come from and then to Pearl. *Shoot.* This was probably illegal, or at least against the rules. But what choice did they have?

Then Eddie noticed them. "Hey," he shouted, dropping the suitcases and running back down the stairs. "Stop! You can't take my cart."

Sally shrieked and jumped into the passenger seat. Eddie leaped through the air to try to block their path. He came up short and landed on one foot, rolling to the side and howling as he grabbed his ankle. Pearl pushed the gas pedal to the floor, whipping Sally's head back as they lurched forward. "Shouldn't we check on Eddie?" Sally said, bracing one hand on the dashboard and the other on the seat between them and looking back to where Eddie was rocking back and forth and speaking into a walkie-talkie.

"You wantin' that Dottie should catch us?" Pearl said with a glance at Sally before she veered off to the right.

Sally shook her head and stared forward, her eyes wide. Pearl was not the best driver. She tended to speed and cut people off. Now she weaved through the resort, shouting at resort guests who ended up in their path. "Move it! We got ourselves a rabid cat on our tail."

A quick swerve to the left, and Sally found herself hanging out of the cart. One arm on the bar was all that kept her from tumbling to the concrete. "Where are you goin'?" Pearl asked.

Sally was stuck. She didn't know if she could pull herself up and didn't want to fall. Her heart was pounding in her ears.

Pearl flew around a corner, and the cart tipped. Sally was thrown upright, her hat soaring like a Frisbee. They veered off the path, bumping over the grass and crashing into a bush.

"Oof!" Sally exclaimed as the cart abruptly stopped.

"Well, shoot," Pearl said, shifting the cart into reverse and flooring the gas pedal.

Sally leaned far over the side and confirmed that one wheel was spinning in the air. She turned around to the front to see bushes tangled in the wheels. She shook her head. "We're stuck."

Pearl banged her hand on the steering wheel and then sucked a breath through her teeth, shaking her hand. "I think I broke my finger."

"Serves you right," Sally said, climbing out of the cart. "We need to get out of here."

"Darn right, we do." Pearl slid her feet to the ground, and they headed to the front of the resort on foot. They slid through a line of trees and followed the dirt path that ran parallel to the road that led in from the front gate.

A security guard was at the gate with a clipboard in hand. When Sally and Pearl approached, Pearl looped her arm through Sally's and said with fake cheeriness, "Just wanna check out some of the local culture and maybe the resort next door." She winked at him. His brown cheeks took on a reddish hue, but he didn't try to stop them.

Once they were outside the gate, Pearl grabbed Sally's arm and pulled her to the left so they couldn't be seen from the main drive. Maybe Dottie would underestimate their willingness to leave the safety of the resort. Hopefully, they could buy some time while she searched the area until she found their crashed cart.

The woman was likely a murderer and knew they were on to her. And even though Sally didn't want to believe it, it was hard to dispute the evidence they had found.

Pearl pulled Sally into a row of tall bushes. She shook her hand. "Ain't broken, just sprained, I think."

Sally nodded, closed her eyes for a moment, and tried to calm her heart rate. "What are we going to do?"

Pearl shook her head and looked up. "I don't know. That woman is nuttier than a porta potty at a peanut festival and she should be locked up. Look how many people she got tangled up in her web, even Mike."

"What makes you think Mike's involved in this?" Sally's face drained of color. That couldn't be possible. Mike was a good guy. She pulled her shoulders back and said, with fake bravado, "There's no way."

Pearl raised one eyebrow. "You sure? Because he seems pretty chummy with that crowd."

Sally pursed her lips and looked at the sky, considering. Then she shook her head again and said, "Not possible. He's a good man. He has kids and grandkids."

Pearl waved her off. "Yeah? So what? Dottie's got grandkids too. Remember she showed us those pictures of that ugly baby?"

"Don't call babies ugly. All babies are beautiful and a gift from God." Sally clenched her fists, the irritation more from the accusations about Mike than the baby comments.

Pearl waved her hand in front of her. "All babies may be a gift from God, but all babies ain't cute." She shook her head and continued. "Why are we talkin' about Dottie's grandchicks? We should be figurin' out what we're gonna do. We got ourselves into a pickle."

"That's the understatement of the year," Sally said, picking a leaf from the bush and ripping it up into little pieces. "Maybe we should just go to the police with the evidence we found."

Pearl stepped out into the road and looked both ways, then took Sally's hand and pulled her onto the sidewalk. "No way. The police did their investigation on the murder, and Dottie is still runnin' free, drinkin' margaritas, and bein' a boil on the butt of humanity. They ain't gonna be any help."

"I think we should at least talk to Mike."

Pearl stopped. "Are you crazy? He'll turn us over to Dottie, and she'll have us dead in our room by tomorrow mornin', and then your daughter will be mad at me for draggin' you down here and gettin' you tangled up with a drug cartel and killed."

Sally looked at her and burst out laughing. The whole thing was ridiculous, and it was precisely what her son had said would happen. Pearl wrinkled her nose and pulled her chin into her neck. Sally let out a deep breath. "Fine."

The sun blazed down on their heads. Sally licked her dry lips. She touched her nose and winced. She was getting sunburned. They walked on, and the road turned to gravel, which kicked up dust with every step they took. Sally shielded her eyes from the sun and peered ahead.

Pearl studied her for a moment and reached out to touch her arm. "You okay?"

"I'm fine," Sally said shakily. "But I'll think twice before booking another vacation with you, just so you know."

Pearl laughed and kicked a rock. "I can't blame you for that." She lifted a foot out in front of her. "Whew, my dogs are barkin'." She moved toward a bench on the side of the road, and Sally gratefully joined Pearl in resting their feet.

They sat in silence for a few minutes, enjoying the quiet. A couple of men walked by, holding hands. Pearl leaned over and whispered, "Ain't they adorable? Look at those tight shorts."

Sally didn't know what to say, so she ignored the comment.

Pearl sat back and patted Sally on the thigh. "Sorry we're in this mess, kid."

Sally covered Pearl's hand and wrapped her fingers around Pearl's. "It's not your fault. Who would've thought a couple of old ladies would end up here?" She looked over and ensured Pearl was looking back at her when she said, "You're my best friend. I am so thankful to know you." Sally's eyes glittered.

"You tryin' to make me cry, Sally?" Pearl pulled her hand back and folded her arms across her chest.

Sally smiled. This was so like Pearl. God forbid she showed any emotions. "I just wanted you to know that I don't blame you for what we're caught up in, and I'm still happy I came. As long as we don't get shot." She wrinkled her nose.

Pearl gave her a sidelong glance. "Well, butter my butt and call me a biscuit. You're glad you're here with me?"

Sally smiled and nodded. "I am. It's an adventure." She wiped the sweat from her brow with the back of her hand. "You know, I would kill for one of those drilled coconuts with a straw."

Pearl pushed herself off the bench and groaned. "Ain't that the truth? I think I punctured a kidney or somethin' in that crash." She poked at her ribs. "Maybe we can sue the resort."

Sally scoffed. "Right. We're gonna sue the resort because we crashed the golf cart we stole?"

Pearl held out a hand to pull Sally up. "Good point. Maybe I'm just gettin' old."

Sally grabbed her hand. "Maybe we're both just getting old."

As Sally stepped forward, a hand covered her mouth and yanked her backward. She couldn't see Pearl, just the road in front of her disappearing as another hand crossed her midsection and pulled her back through the bushes and into the mangrove orchard next to the resort.

Before Sally or Pearl could scream, pillowcases were shoved over their heads. Sally could pick out three different voices as they spoke rapid Spanish. Once again, Sally regretted not having completed her Spanish class. Nausea roiled her stomach. *Oh gosh, I don't want to puke inside a pillowcase.* By the sounds of it, one of the men had his hand over Pearl's mouth. He let out a howl and swore in Spanish.

"Serves you right. I hope I drew blood. Let me go right now!" Pearl demanded. She struggled against the kidnapper holding her arms. "If I had my gun, you'd be sorry."

Sally quickly became disoriented as the men zip-tied her hands in front of her. Pearl was cussing a string of words that would turn a sailor red. She was kicking and hitting anyone within reach, including Sally, who yelped as Pearl's sneaker connected with her shinbone. That was going to leave a bruise.

Sally couldn't see what was going on, but she could hear the scuffling as the men tried to figure out what to do with two old ladies, one of whom was quite unruly. "You let me go," Pearl said. "I'm an American citizen, and they do not take kindly to Americans gettin' kidnapped by foreigners."

"Please," Sally said, "just let us go. Take whatever you want. We won't say anything."

"Oh yes, we will, "Pearl shouted. "We're goin' right to the police, and ya'll are gonna go to jail and then straight to hell."

Sally choked out a cry. Why couldn't Pearl just shut up? She was going to get them both killed. Sally had read all the stories of American tourists getting kidnapped and killed in other countries. She didn't want to die. She couldn't leave her kids orphaned, even if they were adults. Her eyes filled with tears and her nose started to run.

Pearl continued her tirade. The sound of a bottle opening and pouring liquid caused Sally's blood to run cold. Pearl's voice trailed off mid-sentence. What was happening? What had they done to her?

One of the men hissed something Sally couldn't understand, and the ammonia smell filled the air. A hand clapped over the pillowcase and across her mouth. She tried to scream, but the world went dark, and she crumpled to the ground.

42

Kidnapped

When Sally opened her eyes, the pillowcase had been removed. She was lying in the back of a work van. The van was parked, and the driver's seat was empty. She groaned. Her whole body ached. Her mouth tasted like ammonia and was dry as cotton. She rolled onto her back and saw Pearl lying next to her, still unconscious. She tried to shake Pearl awake and realized both of their hands were bound with a black zip ties. Her heart raced with panic. They were going to die. Pearl might already be dead.

Pearl moaned, and her eyes fluttered open. "Are you okay?" Sally asked.

Pearl's voice was scratchy as she found her words. "No, I'm not okay. I'm madder than a wet hen."

Sally smiled despite herself. Pearl was fine. They were both okay for now.

Pearl licked her lips and turned to Sally, "What about you? Are you okay, considerin' the mess we're in??"

Sally nodded.

"Good." Pearl looked up at the roof of the van. "How long

do you think we've been out?"

"I don't know. I have no idea where we are."

Pearl rolled over and up onto her knees. She looked past Sally and out the front windshield. "Looks like we're near a warehouse or somethin'."

"Do you see anybody?"

"Nope. Only some lady sellin' pineapple across the street."

"Can you get her attention?"

"She's too far away, and these windows are tinted."

"What are we going to do?" Sally blinked back tears. She was sure she was in shock. She couldn't feel her leg. It could have been because she was lying on it wrong, but maybe she was wounded somehow. This was awful. Her son had been right. She should never have left home. Harold had been right. Staying home was better. She gulped for air. Her throat was closing up.

Pearl turned to her. "Oh my stars, are you havin' a panic attack? Oh darlin', it's gonna be okay"

"Can't breathe," Sally gasped.

Pearl scooted over on her knees, her eyes wide. "Just breathe. I know things don't look good, but we're gonna get outta this."

Sally shook her head.

" Can you breathe with me?"

Sally nodded. She focused on breathing in through her nose and out through her mouth. Pearl took her hand and breathed with her, purposely slowing down until Sally was no longer gasping. Pearl met her eyes. "It's gonna be okay. I promise. You just gotta try to stay calm."

Sally let her eyes shift away from Pearl, but Pearl reached her bound hands up and grabbed her chin. "No, don't do that. You gotta believe in yourself."

"I don't want to die," Sally mumbled.

"We are not gonna die. We are gonna fight our way out of this. They're gonna be sorry they ever messed with us."

"But what are we going to do?"

Pearl took a deep breath. "I've been in stickier situations than this before." She looked at the zip tie around her hands, turning her wrists from side to side. She pulled them to her mouth, grabbed the end of the zip tie with her teeth, and pulled it tight. Then she raised her hands above her head and brought them down to her stomach. Her arms flapped out like a chicken. The ties snapped apart, and she triumphantly punched the air in front of her.

Sally watched in amazement.

Pearl shook her hands in front of her. "Now let's get you free."

Sally stared down at her zip tied wrists, wondering if she could even do what Pearl had done. "Oh, I don't know." She stretched her wrists apart, the plastic bands digging into her skin. She couldn't see how she would be able to break the bonds.

"You can do this. Just do exactly as I say. Pull it tight with your teeth, then put your hands up over your head."

Sally followed the directions, feeling a bit silly. She wouldn't have believed it was possible if she hadn't just seen Pearl do it.

"Okay, now you gotta do three things at once."

"What?" Sally shook her head, the tightened zip tie digging into her wrists. "I can't do this."

"You gotta. Now listen. Bring your hands down, flap those elbows out, and imagine touching your shoulder blades together." She demonstrated the motions again. "Now you go."

Sally pursed her lips and dropped her hands. Pearl went

through the motion three more times. Sally pursed her lips. Oh, for heaven's sake, it wasn't that complicated. Did she think Sally was an idiot? "Alright, I've got it."

Pearl tilted her head. "Then do it already. I wanna get out of here."

Sally shook her hair off her neck. She took a deep breath and raised her hands over her head. She closed her eyes and whispered a quick prayer. Then she brought her hands down, flapped her elbows, and squeezed her shoulder blades together. Snap. She was free.

Her eyes flew open. Pearl was beaming at her. Sally couldn't believe it. She lifted her hands and inspected her wrists. Angry red lines ringed both of them, but she was free.

"I can't believe it worked." Sally rubbed her wrists.

Pearl pulled her chin into her neck. "Of course it worked. I told you, I took a course at the senior center."

"Now what?" Sally asked, looking around the van.

"We gotta get out of this van." Pearl was already moving to the front of the van. She crawled between the front seats into the passenger side and looked around, using the review mirror to scan the area. "I ain't seein' anyone. Maybe they're inside the house on that side." Pearl pointed out the driver's side window. She cracked open the passenger door, and Sally scrambled to follow. Once they were outside the van, Sally pulled the hem of her shirt down. She sighed as her knees creaked, relieved to be standing.

Pearl waved her on. "Boot, scoot, and boogie already." Sally followed her to the back of the van, where she held up a hand to stop them. There was no sign of the men. There was a two-lane road in front of them and across the street was a colorful billboard advertising a local adventure park. Behind it was the row of warehouses they had seen from the van's tinted window. Pearl pointed. "There, we can hide in there for a minute. I gotta catch my breath."

She grabbed Sally's hand. They waited for a break in the traffic and ran across the road diagonally, away from the houses. The first gray steel warehouse had a door facing the street. Pearl tugged on the handle, but it was locked. They ran around to the north side of the building and found an empty dirt lot and an open bay door. Pearl put an arm up to stop them short at the bay door. Sally opened her mouth to speak, but Pearl shook her head and put a finger to her lips. She dipped her head inside the building and looked around. It was completely silent."Lots of places to hide," Pearl observed. The steel building was two stories tall, with windows around the edges. Inside, pallets of boxes covered the cement floor.

They moved through the boxes until they found one with a shorter stack they could sit on. Pearl pressed down on the stack, making sure it was sturdy. Then she hopped up, leaned against the adjoining stack, and closed her eyes.

Sally climbed up next to her. She tugged on the hem of her shirt and licked her lips. Her mouth and eyes were dry, and her stomach rumbled. How could Pearl be so calm? Sally could hardly breathe. She could barely wrap her mind around what had happened. How had things spun so far out of control?

Pearl's eyes flew open as a car squealed its tires into the parking lot and stopped outside the open bay door. Pearl grabbed Sally's hand, pulling her between some pallets so that they could crouch down out of sight.

43

A Sticky Situation

"Hello, anybody in here?"

Sally's stomach dropped. She knew that voice. The fake pageant queen lilt and carefully crafted newscaster voice. How had Dottie found them so quickly? Where were her crocodile-booted goons?

"Oh my stars," Pearl whispered, rolling her eyes. "How'd she find us?"

Sally pursed her lips, remembering how Dottie had tried to befriend them that first night. The woman was nothing but trouble. What were they going to do? Sally turned to look behind them. Spotting a door in the corner, she whispered, "We're going to have to make a run for it."

"I can hear you talking. You're not that quiet," Dottie called out.

Sally hadn't heard her voice among the kidnappers, but she must have been involved if she found them so quickly. Sally strained to hear where Dottie was in the warehouse. They needed to get away from her, but how? If they wanted to get to the door, they would have to cross a wide opening between the stacks of boxes. If they ran they could reach it. But if the door was locked, they were sunk.

Maybe they should give up. Maybe they could talk to her and reason with Dottie, considering everything she had on the line. Sally locked her knees together and bit her lip. Who was she kidding? They couldn't reason with that woman. Dottie had already proven she would kill to get what she wanted.

"You can come out. It's okay. This was all just a misunderstanding." Dottie's voice was further away than it had been before.

"Misunderstandin'?" Pearl hissed. "Ain't no misunderstandin'. She is one number short of a bingo, like I said."

Sally nodded. Their best chance for escape was to run. She squeezed Pearl's hand and pointed to the door. Pearl gave her a quick nod. Sally leaned close to Pearl's ear, "Let's go. On the count of three."

"Come on, girls, let's grab a drink and talk it out."

Sally put up her fingers.

One.

Two.

Three.

Sally took a deep breath and ran, pulling Pearl along after her. They crossed between two pallets of boxes. "Hey," Dottie called out from the other side of the building.

"She saw us," Pearl panted as they ran.

"Keep moving," Sally said without looking back.

"If I have a heart attack, I'm gonna kill you."

A loud crack rang out, and glass rained from a window above. They both shrieked, Sally's ears ringing. "What was that?" she asked.

"Gunshot."

Sally's steps faltered, but Pearl grabbed her elbow and pulled her along. A gunshot? Sally had never heard a gunshot in real life.

"Faster," Pearl cried. They were twenty feet from the door. Another gunshot hit a stack of boxes next to them.

"She shoots like a hippie," Pearl said.

Sally ran full speed into the door and threw her body against it, bursting into the sunlight.

They slammed the door behind them. Sally frantically looked around for something to jam the door. Old trailers and rusted cars littered the dirt lot next to the warehouse. She moved to grab a shovel leaning against the wall when two gunshots blew a hole clean through the door and pinged off an old Chevy. Sally and Pearl both jumped.

"Dumb hippie's aim's gettin' better," Pearl said, grabbing Sally's arm and running, "We gotta get outta here."

They ran, crossing back over the street and into the residential area where the van had been parked. If they were lucky, they could lose Dottie and make a plan. They were three blocks in when Pearl slowed to a walk to catch her breath.

"Where are we?" Sally asked, looking for anything she recognized as they moved.

Pearl squinted her eyes and surveyed the landscape. "Don't know. But if we head away from the sun, we're bound to hit the beach and a resort with someone in it who speaks English."

Sally nodded. That was smart. If they could find someone who spoke English, they would be okay.

Pearl nodded, and they wove through the buildings and small houses dotting the landscape. They rounded the corner of a half-built cinder block home and were met by a snarling black dog at the end of a heavy chain. Pearl shrieked as the growling dog jumped at her before being yanked back as the chain tautened. Sally's hand flew to her chest. Saved by the industrial-strength stake driven into the ground, they both jumped back and ran just outside the chain's radius.

They cut between houses, dodging clotheslines and a group of little kids playing soccer. When Sally saw them, she immediately thought of her own children. She would not leave them orphaned because of some drug-dealing witch.

They continued alternating between walking and jogging, albeit more walking than jogging considering how winded they were. But they kept an eye out, determined to make it back to the safety of the Nueva Vida del Mar and demand that the resort manager call the police.

The road taking them in the direction of the beach ended at a street parallel to the coast. Sally remembered that this was the road with resort entrances on it. They were close.

"Left or right?" Pearl said, surveying the options.

Sally peered in both directions trying to remember anything from when they had arrived. She had no idea but said a quick prayer and guessed. "Left."

They headed north, and a block up, there was a white block building with advertisements in the windows and an awning over the door. A store. "Maybe someone in there speaks English?" Sally said, pointing to the building.

"Doubt it. But good gravy, I could use a drink." Unfortunately, the kidnappers had taken their phones and purses.

Sally was staring longingly at the store, her mouth dry with thirst, when the two men in crocodile boots walked out of the door. Toothpick Guy saw them first and jabbed his partner on the arm, pointing in their direction. Then he pulled out his phone and dialed a number.

"Oh crap," Sally said, pulling Pearl around the corner, and they took off again. She didn't want to wait around to see who he was calling.

Sally could have cried when she saw the sign above the entrance to their resort. They rounded the corner onto the narrow drive and kept going. They couldn't see far behind or in front of them because of the winding path.

The sound of shouting and footsteps followed them. Sally's heart beat loudly in her ears, and all she could think about was the gun strapped to that man's side. As if on cue, a gunshot rang out. Sally screamed. Why were they getting shot at again?

"Weave while you run," Pearl huffed out.

"What?"

"Oprah said so!"

Sally didn't have the time or breath to ask for more information, so she started weaving along with Pearl. She tripped on a rock, stumbling forward, her arms flailing and dust filling her eyes, hands out in case she had to break her fall. Pearl grabbed her elbow and tugged her backward. "Good gravy, don't go sprainin' an ankle now."

Her entire body screamed at her to stop. Finally, the drive straightened out for a bit. They were halfway to the resort if she remembered correctly. Behind them, another gunshot rang out. Sally looked back over her shoulder and saw the two men getting closer. And they weren't alone.

44

Shots Fired

Crocodile boots slapped against the pavement as the men closed the distance with grim determination. And between the two men, her face twisted in anger, was Dottie.

"Faster," Sally sputtered in between breaths.

"I can't go any faster. I'm gonna have a heart attack."

Sally could see the blue concrete of the tennis courts off to the left through the bushes. Beyond that, she knew there were maintenance buildings. Maybe they could hide there or find someone to help. If they didn't get off this path, they were done for. She grabbed Pearl's hand and yanked her through the bushes.

"Ouch," Pearl said, branches scraping her face and arms.

"Shhh. We need to find somewhere to hide."

They ducked between the tall bushes lining the tennis court and the chain link fence. A tennis ball smacked against the ground echoed by the grunts of the two men they had seen holding hands earlier. Now they were dripping with sweat and so wrapped up in their game that they didn't notice Sally and Pearl slinking past, heading for the building. "We should ask them for help," Sally said.

"And get 'em shot?" Pearl said, shaking her head.

Sally considered. She would feel awful if something were to happen to them simply because they were trying to help. She pressed her lips closed and stayed quiet as they crept out of the tennis players' earshot, continuing towards the maintenance buildings. As they slipped out of the bushes, a voice called out from the right.

"Sally, what are you..." Mike was striding towards them, a frown on his face and his brows furrowed with worry.

Sally paused, waving her arms in front of her. "Stop."

He quickly scanned the area and then asked, "Are you okay? I've been looking everywhere for you. Where's Pearl?"

Sally frantically looked around and didn't see her. Maybe Pearl had run ahead. She grabbed his hand and pulled him around the side of the maintenance building. Pearl was climbing onto the front bumper of a rusty Impala parked next to the dumpster. "I heard gunshots and called the police. They're on their way. What's going on?" Mike asked, shielding his eyes and staring at Pearl's haphazard scrambling.

Sally shook her head. Her mouth was dry as sawdust as she tried to catch her breath. There was no quick way to explain. She wouldn't even know where to start.

Pearl spoke up. "Dottie is fixin' to kill us just like she killed Chuck. Now get over here and gimme a boost. We gotta hide." Pearl stood on the hood of the Impala, lifting her leg in an effort to get herself over the side and into the green metal dumpster.

"Oh geez," Mike said. Pearl was going to kill herself before Dottie got the chance to. As Sally and Mike hustled over to stop Pearl from tumbling into the trash heap, Dottie and the crocodile-booted men rounded the corner.

"What do we have here?" Dottie asked as she slowed to a walk. Her eyes were wild, but she hadn't even broken a sweat. Somehow her hair was still perfectly teased on top, and her bright pink lipstick remained intact. She looked like a deranged Marie Antoinette.

Mike and Sally stopped short of reaching Pearl and turned to face Dottie.

"Dottie, what's all this about?" Mike asked.

"Mike, this has nothing to do with you," Dottie said.

Pearl had one leg hooked over the side of the dumpster. "I told you. Dottie here is fixin' to kill us just like she killed Chuck."

"Shut up, you southern trash," Dottie said.

Mike held his hands in front of him defensively and said in an even tone, "Now, everyone just needs to calm down."

Sally looked at Mike. What was he doing? Maybe he could diffuse the situation, but it was not likely with hot-headed Dottie holding a gun.

"That's all I need, another man telling me to calm down." Dottie let her arms drop to her sides and set her jaw. "Chuck tried that, too. He thought he could push me out as leader of the Flamingo Singles, the group I started, and then was surprised when I got upset. He had no respect for all the work I put in. He just thought he could cut me out of the deal." She shook her head, "And you, why did you have to be such a boy scout, Mike? If you weren't such a prude, we could have made a lot of money together."

Dottie turned to the men wearing crocodile boots, who were catching their breath and wiping sweat off their brows with handkerchiefs they had fished from their pockets. "What are you doing?" She waved her gun toward Sally and Pearl. "Take care of them."

"The usual spot?" Mr. Friendly asked.

"Where else, crap-for-brains?" Dottie spat, waving her gun around.

The men gave a slight nod. Then began stalking closer and lifting their guns.

Dottie shielded her eyes with her hand. "Sorry, Mike. Wrong place at the wrong time." She shrugged.

As the men moved forward, Sally ran over to Pearl and pulled her down from the dumpster. Mike was right there with her, standing between Sally and Dottie and making sure Pearl didn't crash to the ground. In the distance, sirens wailed. The men paused at the sound.

"It's too late, Dottie," Mike said, turning back to look at her once Pearl was on the ground and standing behind him next to the Impala.

Dottie let out an exasperated wail. "Why are you ruining everything?" Seething, her eyes dug into Sally. "This is all your fault."

Sally's throat bobbed. Mike took Sally's elbow and pulled her behind him. "Don't blame Sally for this."

Sally stared at the ground between Mike's feet. No man had ever stuck up for her this way. Pearl grabbed her hand and squeezed.

"You need to move," Dottie said between gritted teeth.

"Come on, Dottie. Put the gun down and let's talk."

"Don't act like you're interested in talking to me, now. It's obvious you only want her."

Sally's face flamed. She didn't dare look up. Pearl choked back a laugh. Sally elbowed her, and Pearl covered her laugh with a cough.

As the sirens grew closer, Toothpick Guy and Mr. Friendly looked at each other and then turned to run. "Hey! Get back here," Dottie called out after them, to no effect. She swore and turned her attention back to Mike. "I will shoot you."

Mike took a step backward and swore under his breath.

Sally let her eyes rise enough to look over Mike's shoulder. Dottie had her gun pointed directly at him. Would she actually shoot Mike? How could this be happening?

Dottie cocked the gun, and the sound stopped Sally's breath.

Mike rushed Dottie, whose eyes went wide with surprise. As he moved he yelled, "Get down" to Sally and Pearl. Sally willed her feet to move, but they refused to cooperate.

As Dottie squeezed the trigger, Mike pushed her arms to the side and the bullet hit the Impala, smashing the windshield. Dottie screeched as they wrestled for the gun.

Before she could think, Sally rushed forward to help. Dottie pulled at the gun with both hands, hatred searing across her features as she fired wildly in Sally's direction. Suddenly Sally's body was twisting, her left arm screaming with the pain of impact as a bullet tore through fabric and skin. She stumbled, losing her footing. Dottie's maniacally grinning face gave way to blue sky, and then pavement as she fell, failing to brace herself with an injured and uncooperative arm. She ended up doing an awkward tuck and roll, grunting and moaning as she made painful contact with the pavement.

Mike yelled, "Sally!" Then he gave Dottie a hard shove to the ground and ripped the gun from her hands.

"Oh no!" Pearl said, running to Sally's side.

"Check for bleeding," Mike said, keeping the gun trained on Dottie.

"I know that. You just keep that evil woman on the ground."

239

The footsteps on the pavement filled her ears as she moaned and closed her eyes. She was going to die. She had been shot, and she was going to die right now. It wasn't fair. She was just finding her way forward. She wasn't ready to die. Her thoughts were drowned out by approaching sirens. Pearl's face swam in and out of focus above her, contorted with worry and demanding she stay awake. She tried to form words but stared at the blue sky and watched a white puffy cloud pass across her field of vision. She flattened herself out, the concrete making contact with her entire body.

"The police are here, and medics are on the way." It was Mike talking to her now, brushing her hair back. "Just stay with me."

45

Have Fun in Jail

"She's bleeding," Pearl said, and Sally could feel her tugging at her sleeve.

"It just grazed her. Keep pressure on it. She'll be okay," Mike said.

Sally struggled to focus her thoughts. Where was Dottie? Did she get away? Maybe Dottie was dead. Why couldn't she make herself ask? Maybe she was in shock. She was so tired. Was she dying? She didn't feel like she was dying. And anyone would be tired after all the running they had done. She closed her eyes and let herself rest. Mike took off his sweatshirt and rolled it, placing it under her feet. He and Pearl held her hands until the medics arrived.

"This is all my fault," Pearl said through tears. "I should never have brought you here."

Sally could hear her but only had the energy to squeeze her hand.

Then paramedics were on the scene. They examined her quickly, determining she wasn't seriously injured, and then helped her to the back of the ambulance. She flinched as they slipped a syringe of pain medicine into her right arm. Then they cleaned and glued shut the gash in her left arm. Pearl was beside her, fussing and insisting on cleaning the wounds on her skinned knees.

Mike was standing with a small group of police officers, his worried gaze flitting to Sally every few moments. Then he pulled out his phone and talked intensely to someone on the other end. Sally watched him, flinching from the pressure of Pearl's hand on her throbbing knee. She didn't even remember skinning them, she'd been so focused on the intensity of the last few hours. Where was Dottie? Where were the men? Surely they didn't get away?

Pearl finished bandaging her knees and swung around to sit next to her on the gurney. "What happened after I was shot?" Sally asked Pearl.

Pearl took a deep breath. "It all happened faster than a knife fight in a phone booth."

"Where's Dottie?" Sally asked, shaken.

Pearl pointed with the gauze in her hand to a cop car. Sally squinted. Dottie was sitting in the back, head hanging down, her lips moving as if she was talking to someone.

"They arrested her?"

Pearl leaned over and met her eyes. "Did you hit your head? Of course they arrested her. She tried to kill you. And they dragged those crooked, crocodile-wearin' cops away already."

Sally tried to remember the details. If Mike hadn't stopped her, Dottie would've killed her and Pearl. Her eyes landed on Mike, who looked fine. She sighed in relief.

Sally slid off the stretcher and climbed down out of the ambulance. Her teeth rattled when her feet hit the ground.

"Where are you goin'?" Pearl asked, her brows knitted

together.

Sally didn't respond. She headed straight for the cop car Dottie was sitting in. She needed answers.

Dottie was leaning back now, her eyes closed. When Sally rapped on the window, Dottie's cuffed hands jumped in surprise.

Dottie's left eye was a swollen purple mess. She narrowed her right eye and asked, "What do you want?"

Sally swallowed. She wanted to understand how Dottie ended up being such a horrible person. She wanted to know how things spun so far out of control. Maybe it was her true crime affinity, but she wanted closure. "Why did you do it?"

Dottie huffed. "You'll need to be more specific."

Sally stood up straight and folded her arms. Who did Dottie think she was? She was in cuffs in the back of a car and still had an attitude.

Dottie raised her hands and pushed the hair out of her eyes. "Get me some water."

Sally instinctively turned to find some water for Dottie, then paused. What was she doing? She was tired of being told what to do. And she wasn't going out of her way for this sociopath. She turned around and quietly said, "No."

Dottie's face burned with rage, and she spat, "You know, you think you're all high and mighty, but all you did was make sure a bunch of wonderful seniors lost their jobs. They will be destitute, and it is all your fault."

Sally smiled. She wasn't taking the bait. "What happened to your face?"

Dottie straightened her shoulders and looked forward. "Why don't you ask Pearl? I'm planning to press charges against her for assault."

"Did she punch you?" Pearl hadn't said anything. Had she hurt her hand?

"Yes. She just proved I was right about her being southern trash."

Sally smiled as she imagined Pearl hauling off and punching Dottie. "You deserved it. How many people have you recruited to be murderers?"

Dottie turned to her and scoffed. "Murderers? Please. They were employed to help move items across the border."

"Oh, items like the rollaway full of heroin in your room? So the Flamingo Singles are actually a front for drug running. Classy. Is Mike a part of that?"

Dottie shook her hair and scoffed. "Mike is a liar and a terrible person. He pretended to be one of us but turned out to be a snitch."

"A what?" Sally asked, looking at Mike again.

"A snitch. A cop."

Sally looked at Dottie, who nodded in confirmation, and then back to Mike. Was Mike a police officer? What was he doing in Mexico? Now she had questions for him. She turned to Dottie again. "I thought beauty queens were supposed to want peace on earth. If that's what you were going for, you suck at it."

She turned and walked away. Behind her, Dottie shouted and kicked the seat in front of her. Sally ignored her.

Mike and Pearl turned to her as she approached. "You okay?" he asked, frowning.

"I'm fine."

"That woman ain't got the good sense God gave a rock." Pearl lifted her chin in the direction of Dottie, who was still pitching a fit in the back of the cop car.

"So, you're a cop?" Sally asked Mike.

He shuffled his feet, put his hands on his hips, and said, "Yes."

"What?" Pearl said, her mouth agape.

"How did you get mixed up with Dottie?" Sally asked, meeting his gaze and holding it.

He smirked. "You make a good interrogator."

"And you make a good liar."

Mike drew back as if she had slapped him. Sally didn't know where that tone had come from. But she was embarrassed. She had trusted him. And he'd never thought to tell her the truth?

He dropped his hands to his sides. "I am sorry about that. I've been working on this case for months. As you probably figured out, Dottie has been running a drug smuggling ring under the banner of her Flamingo Singles. I have been working with the Mexican drug police and was getting close to enough evidence for a conviction. And then you two showed up. I tried to get you to stay away from her. You didn't need to be mixed up in this mess."

"Too late," Pearl huffed, folding her arms.

"What happens now?" Sally asked as a paramedic handed her an open water bottle. She took a long drink.

"The corrupt cops have been arrested. Shannon and Ricky have been picked up and will testify against Dottie. I suppose they'll be extradited to the U.S. and serve some time. And you know where Dottie is." He pointed to the police car parked by the entrance to the resort.

"You should search her room. We found drugs in her suitcase, remember Sally?" Pearl asked.

Mike nodded. "We are searching her room now."

"Suitcase, back of the closet behind the shoes," Sally offered.

"It's been quite a day." Mike put his hand on her uninjured

arm and met her eyes. "I am so sorry you're hurt."

"She solved your case is what she did," Pearl interjected.

Mike chuckled and folded his arms. "She sure did." Then he turned to Sally. "Thank you."

Sally smiled. "You're welcome. Someone's having a hissy fit." She lifted her chin in Dottie's direction.

They all turned to Dottie, who was still shouting indignantly and thrashing around in the back of the cop car.

"She'd better get comfortable. It'll be a while before she gets another vacation in the sun," Mike said.

"She's goin' to be more upset about the roots, wrinkles, and orange jumpsuit in her future," Pearl said.

46

Better Than Okay

As soon as Sally, Pearl, and Mike walked through the restaurant doors, the murmuring began. It was clear that news of Dottie's arrest had spread. Sally's arm was sore, but they had given her some pain medication to take the edge off. All she wanted to do was crawl into bed, but Mike insisted they get some food in them first. She suspected he was also watching them for signs of distress after everything that had happened.

While Sally shrank away from the gaping mouths and curious glances, Pearl preened like a peacock, enjoying their notoriety, smiling at gawking guests as they passed. Sally smiled, glad to have Pearl take the spotlight.

She wasn't sure she could eat. Adrenaline still coursed through her, quashing her appetite. When the server set down a bowl of warm chips and a selection of mild salsas in front of her, though, an audible rumbling came from her midsection. Pearl reached out to pull the basket closer to her, and Sally instinctively wrapped her fingers around the edge of the wicker to stop her. She was starving. When had they last eaten? Had it been just this morning that they had shared room service?

Pearl frowned. Mike waved over their server and asked for another set of chips and salsa. Pearl smiled at him and ordered a margarita. Sally licked her lips. She would have loved one but wasn't sure about mixing alcohol with the pain medication, so she ordered an iced tea instead.

Their conversation was limited by exhaustion and chewing. The rush from earlier began to wear off. Sally found herself propping her chin up with her good arm and letting her eyes flutter shut until she began to lean dangerously over the edge of the table, startling herself awake.

After the meal, Mike walked them out of the restaurant, where they were greeted by Eddie, ankle in a boot cast, waiting for them in another golf cart. Sally was mortified, and even Pearl blanched. But Eddie just smiled a toothy grin.

Mike motioned to the cart. "Ladies, I think you have done enough walking for today. Eddie here is going to give you a ride." He gave them a small salute. "I have to take care of some business. I'll check in later."

Sally shifted on her feet. She was pretty sure she wouldn't make it back to their room if they had to walk, but poor Eddie.

"Come on," Pearl said, "Unless you expect me to throw you over my shoulder and carry you."

Sally resisted the urge to giggle as she pictured Pearl fireman-carrying her up the stairs. A ride with Eddie seemed to be the best option, even if she felt terrible about what had happened earlier and was shocked at his good humor, considering. As she climbed on the back of the cart, Sally said, "Oh gosh, we are so sorry, Eddie."

Eddie smiled, "It's okay. I will tell all my friends I was part of a crime fight." He held his ankle up. "No breaks. It will be fine. And Mr. Mike made it better with a huge tip."

Sally reached up and put a hand on his shoulder. "Thank you." He nodded and turned to face forward in the driver's seat.

"He's takin' it pretty darn well," Pearl observed.

"Surprisingly well. You'll have to go back to that travel website and give him a good review."

Pearl snapped her fingers. "Hot dog, that's exactly what I'm gonna do."

They rode the rest of the way to their room in silence. The sidewalks were mostly empty in the lull between dinner and the evening entertainment.

Sally had never been so happy to shut the door to their room and turn the deadbolt. The freshly made crisp white sheets were calling her name. She was sticky, dirty, and pretty sure she smelled. "I need a shower."

"You go. I'll hop in next. Make sure you put that waterproof bandage on your arm first. Don't need it gettin' infected."

Sally dug into her pocket for the square bandage, waved it in Pearl's direction, and headed towards the bathroom.

Pearl sat on the edge of the bed, staring at her hands. "Hey, Sally?"

Sally stopped and turned back to her. "Yeah?"

"I ain't got too many people in my life I can count on." She looked up at Sally. "Don't think I would've made it today without you."

Sally smiled at her friend. "You can always count on me. Just like I can count on you to punch trigger-happy pageant queens and get me out of trouble"

Pearl wiped her eye. "Yeah." Then she pointed at Sally. "Don't go thinkin' I'm gettin' all soft and needy."

"Not a chance," Sally said, smiling. She turned and walked

through the bathroom door, exhaling deeply. Pearl could handle a drug cartel without a problem, but sharing her feelings took a heroic effort. Sally was proud of her friend.

In the shower, she carefully washed her hair. Every inch of her body ached, especially her arm underneath the waterproof bandage. Looking at the bruises from her fall forming on her leg, she was reminded that over the next few days, everything would hurt worse before it got better. Luckily she had more pain medication to get her home.

Home. It would be heavenly to sleep in her own bed. And she missed her sunflower kitchen. Had Lauren remembered to water her plants? Her daughter would have a million questions. How would she explain this to her kids?

It turned out she never needed to worry. When it was Pearl's turn in the shower, Lauren called. "Oh, thank God. Mom, are you okay? You were on the news," Lauren shrieked through the phone.

The news? How could that be?

"I'm fine. Why was I on the news?"

"Henry saw it online and called me. I didn't believe him, so I turned on the news and there you were. They said two senior women had busted an international drug ring. They even had a picture of you and Pearl at the scene. You were sitting in the back of an ambulance. Are you sure you're okay? They said you'd been shot."

"I was. The bullet grazed my arm." Sally looked down at her bandaged arm. "I think it's going to leave a cool scar. Honestly, the worst pain is in my sore feet." She wiggled her toes, which were propped up on pillows, her ankles swollen from the day's activities.

"What do you mean by 'grazed?' Are you in the hospital?"

"Settle down. I'm perfectly capable of caring for myself." She reached for the water on the nightstand and let the cool glass sit on her lips for a beat. "Make sure your worrywart brother Joel saw the story. Send him the link if he hasn't. He needs to know he was right about Mexico but wrong about me."

"Mom? I don't even know what to say. I'm so glad you're okay. It's all that matters to me, but-" Lauren's words wavered huskily over the phone. "I always knew you were strong. I always thought you could take on the world if you ever actually had to. So why do I feel like I'm hearing your real voice for the first time right now?"

"I guess that old armchair muffled it pretty badly, but it's always been there. Thanks for hearing it, honey. I'll be home tomorrow and can tell you everything, loud and clear."

"You'd better. I want to hear every detail. You're sure you're okay?"

Sally held her breath before confidently answering, "So much better than okay."

47

A New Day

Thursday, October 21st

After a night of peaceful sleep, Sally rolled out of bed and tiptoed to the bathroom. Pearl was still snoring in the next bed and mumbling something about tequila, which made Sally swallow a giggle.

The sun was beginning to push back the darkness. Perfect, she thought, pulling on a sweatshirt over her cotton pajama set and slipping on her brown leather sandals. Watching the sunrise over the ocean had always been on Sally's bucket list. After a quick swish of mouthwash and pulling a brush through her hair, she headed out.

The grass was frosted with dew in the quiet courtyard. Exterior lamps still cast pots of yellow light onto the sidewalk. She was caught in the blur between night and day, that strange in-between that most of the world was never awake to enjoy. She smiled to herself.

The waves lapped at the shore in the distance, growing louder as she followed the path to where it met the beach. She abandoned her sandals and embraced the coolness of the sand between her toes.

The beach was quiet. The staff hadn't yet started raking the seaweed, a gift from every high tide that ended up being carted to a far-off corner of the resort and dumped into a large pile. The pelicans were already finding purchase on the rocks rimming the swimming area. Tipping her head back, Sally surveyed the sky, stars still visible to the west and color continuing to break to the east.

If she had all the time in the world, she didn't think she would be able to describe to someone just how beautiful it was. Heaven seemed so close and she was keenly aware of how small she was in the universe. Her heart was full of wonder and something like gratitude. She breathed in the salt air through her nose and knew that she was exactly where she needed to be. She picked her way around the seaweed until her toes touched the smooth outline of the last wave on the sand. A breeze caught her hair, and she shivered and shoved her hands into the pockets of her sweatshirt. The fingers of her left hand slid cleanly against each other, a strange sensation she wasn't used to yet. Last night she had removed her wedding ring for the last time and carefully placed it in the pocket of her purse. Maybe she would pick up a fashion ring to wear instead.

Behind her, a deep voice said warmly, "Good morning."

Sally turned to see Mike wearing gym shorts and a sweatshirt. He was holding a steaming cup of coffee and grinning at her.

"You're up early," she said, turning to face him, pushing a strand of hair behind her ear.

He nodded. "You too."

"I just wanted to see the sunrise."

He lifted his chin. "You picked a perfect morning for it."

Sally smiled. "I know. It's amazing."

Mike's eyes moved to her injury. "How's your arm?"

Sally looked down at where the bandage was under her sleeve and said, "Not bad. Pearl says it will leave a cool scar. I told my daughter so, too."

Mike shifted on his feet. "I was planning to go for a walk down the beach. Would you like to join me?"

Sally's mouth went dry. Despite all she had been through, doubt clouded her eyes. Scanning the beach, she realized just how alone they were. Would anyone even hear her if she screamed? Her hand went to her throat, and she met Mike's gaze.

He tipped his head to the side, laughter in his eyes. "It's just a walk. And you are welcome to decline."

She pushed down the insecurities. The thing was, she didn't want to decline. Something about Mike made her heart flutter. She liked him and felt safe with him around.

She looked at her feet and then back up at him. "Okay."

He smiled and held his coffee cup out in the direction he was proposing to go. They fell into step and comfortable silence. The gulls began to call out as they made low passes over the water and then lifted to soar above the beach before swinging around for another pass.

"So..." Sally began and then trailed off. She wasn't sure what she wanted to say. She snuck a sideways glance at him. He was watching her, but she couldn't read his expression. She struggled to find words she could string into a decent sentence. "Um.. so... were you actually in the military?"

"Yes. I joined the military when I turned eighteen, mostly to escape our small town," he shrugged. "I've been on the road ever since."

"Were you ever married?"

He sipped his coffee and then said, "I was married once. We were young." He took another sip of coffee, and Sally didn't speak even though she had a million questions. "We met in the army. We were both stationed in Oklahoma. She was killed in a training exercise."

"Oh, I am so sorry."

Mike smiled sadly. "It was a long time ago. I never remarried. Life's been good to me overall, though. I have wonderful kids and grandkids."

They stopped and faced each other. The sun was above the horizon, glowing orange across the water and onto the beach. It was one of those romantic moments Sally had seen in movies but never experienced, and it took her breath away.

Time seemed to pause, just for them. Mike's eyes softened. He looked at her mouth, then back at her eyes. Warmth spread through her midsection. He leaned in. He was going to kiss her. Part of her wanted him to, with his blue eyes sparkling and his tongue passing softly over the gentle curve of his lips.

Everything slowed down, and she watched his eyes close as his face moved nearer. Her eyes widened with fear. She didn't want this, at least not now. She was just getting her own life back. Instinctively she took a step backward.

When Mike leaned over his center of gravity and found only air, he fell forward, his eyes flying open in surprise. Sally gasped as he caught himself before falling. "What's wrong?"

Sally was mortified. She grabbed his hand. "I'm so sorry, Mike."

Mike laughed uncomfortably and raked his hand through his hair. "Jeez, Sally, I'm the one who's sorry. I thought you wanted me to kiss you."

"I did," she said and then looked down. "But I don't."

Mike put his hand on his hips. "I wish I understood."

Sally inhaled deeply. "I was married for 46 years. This is the first chance I've had to just be me. I really like that person, and I want to get to know her better before I jump into someting new."

Mike sighed and nodded in reluctant understanding.

"Mike, you are a wonderful man. I can't think of anyone better if I was looking for, um..." Her face flushed with embarrassment, and she threw her arms in front of her, gesturing to him. "But I'm not, right now." Sally dropped her arms to her sides.

Mike shook his head and chuckled. "You continue to surprise me, Sally."

Sally knew she was making the right choice but didn't want to hurt his feelings. "I'm sorry."

Mike held his hands up before him. "Don't apologize. There's no need." Then he touched her cheek. "I see you. I see the woman you have always been, but have been forced to hide for whatever reason. And you are lovely. Promise me you won't let that happen again. You deserve to stand in the light."

Sally put her hand over his, her eyes filling with tears. He did see her. "Thank you." She turned her head and looked back towards the resort. "I should get back to Pearl. Our flight leaves in a few hours, and I promised to bring her coffee this morning."

"Of course. You two have a special friendship. I'm kind of envious."

As Sally neared the edge of the beach, a familiar, potentially offensive embroidered hat came into view. "Figured you were tied up, so I done went ahead and got the coffee," Pearl said, holding up a pair of to-go cups. They were labeled "Good Cop" and "Bad Cop" with a sharpie, and she held them both toward Sally, letting her choose.

"Gotta admit," Pearl said, as Sally took the "Bad Cop" coffee cup, "I'm kinda disappointed that you weren't Fifty Shades of tied up, if you know what I mean."

"I'm not disappointed," Sally said, linking arms with Pearl. "Getting untied is the best thing that ever happened to me. After meeting you, I guess."

"Gettin' mushy!" Pearl spluttered, holding up her "Good Cop" coffee cup as though to shield herself from sentimentality.

"Being honest," Sally answered, taking a sip of her coffee before raising it as if to toast. "Here's to Mexico, and my best friend."

"Best friend? Shoot, better not tell me who she is or there's gonna be another murder on this resort to reckon with!"

Peals of mutual laughter mingled with the cresting waves and the calling gulls. Sally's heart was full, and although they were going home, she had the feeling this was just the beginning of their adventures together.

THE END

Acknowledgment

This book was inspired by a trip to Mexico in 2021 with my good friend Laurie McGuire. We actually did name pelicans and had the best waitress named Sue. We also met a delightful couple that inspired Shannon and Ricky in all the best ways.

The book wouldn't have been possible without the support of my family and friends. I am thankful for my wonderful beta readers and proofreaders, whose valuable feedback made the story so much better. A special thanks to Alexis A. Wright for her excellent editing and proofreading skills.

The main characters, Sally and Pearl, were named after my grandma and great-grandma. These women were instrumental in making me who I am today. Their love is a legacy worth honoring, and it has been fun breathing life into their namesakes.

I want to thank God for giving me this season of life to write. It is the fulfillment of a lifelong dream that I could not have achieved without the loving support of my husband Kevin, and my family.

Also by Wendy Day

Meet the Author....

Wendy Day writes Urban Fantasy, Contemporary Women's Fiction, and Dystopian stories featuring snappy dialogue, complex relationships, and closed-door romance. She lives in Michigan with her supportive husband, four children, two cats, and two dogs. When she isn't writing, you might find her floating in the lake or with a pole in the water, fishing. She loves sunny autumn days, the first snow of the season, and curling up by the fire with a good book.

Find out more at www.ReadWendyDay.com

WENDY DAY

STANDING WATER

Standing Water

She survived the collapse of America. Now she just wants to live.

Nineteen-year-old Jamie dreams of adventure far from the small town where her family took refuge during the virus and subsequent war of 2027. Ten years later, the country is beginning to rebuild, and she even has a map hanging on her bedroom wall with push-pin plans.

But when her dad is suddenly dragged out of their farmhouse by government officials, Jamie's world is rocked again. Her mom is in denial, and her little brother looks to her for answers.

Can she rescue her father and protect the town she is so eager to escape? Or will this adventure cost her everything?

Killing Cupid

We need to talk about your aim...

For Callie Mcguire, love is that mysterious, magical thing you read about in books. It's Darcy's and Elizabeth Bennet's passionate romance: beautiful, bittersweet, and inspiring.

And it's entirely out of reach.

Callie moved all the way to Chicago to find love, and it's been failure after failure. Almost ready to give up on the notion, she stumbles across a new dating website with an incredible promise: true love with a million-dollar satisfaction guarantee.

Determined to make this her last attempt at finding her match, Callie signs up. When the results turn out to be nothing like she expected, she decides to call the whole thing off and abandon romance for a while.

Little does she know that her decisions will send her life in a direction she never could have expected, and she's forced to realize that perhaps Cupid has a little more influence in our love lives than we thought.

Hera's Revenge
A curse as old as time...

At 24 years old, Kat Phillips has a stable job, an apartment, and her favorite taco place on speed dial. She should be happy, but she's not. When she realizes her life might be stuck in neutral forever, Kat goes into full panic mode. She jumps in her car and heads south to the one person who she knows will understand.

With her grandmother's advice comes revelations that rock Kat's world. Generational secrets come to light and a shocking possibility sends Kat on a thrilling search for answers before her next birthday.

The clock is ticking. With her life on the line and handsome, mysterious Jace Woods tempting her heart, Kat will have to challenge fate and change her destiny.

Made in United States
Orlando, FL
17 December 2022

26960765R00161